THE
LOCKHART
BREED

THE LOCKHART BREED

T.V. Olsen

WALKER AND COMPANY
NEW YORK

JH

First published in the United States of America in 1967 by Berkley Medallion Books.

This edition published in 1982 by the Walker Publishing Company, Inc.

ISBN: 0-8027-4006-5

Library of Congress Catalog Card Number: 81-70967

Printed in the United States of America

10 9 8 7 6 5 4 3 2 1

CHAPTER ONE

Pressed against the raw slope on his belly, Poe watched the rider come on across the hot and dismal flat. He saw the man reach the base of the slope well below his position, and pull up there and dismount. A sunglint raced off the barrel of the Winchester the man drew from its scabbard before thumbing back his hat and turning up his face to the flank of the vast hogback looming above him.

Rydell himself, Poe thought. *Well, I'm damned.* He'd heard that Rydell had been hired to head up the gang of Pimas that tracked Coldrock's escaped convicts, and he might have guessed, from the way his trail had been dogged all this time by only one rider, that his lone pursuer would be Tom Rydell, former U. S. deputy marshal.

Poe Lockhart lay sideways on the slope behind one of the massive boulders that studded this bare, isolated promontory where he had sought cover because he could go no farther and because the flinty ground would temporarily baffle a tracker's eye. He had needed a few minutes to rest and think, but already his time was up.

He turned his head a few inches, his raw-lidded eyes grating in their sockets. His face was rocky-featured and pleasantly ugly at its best, with faintly batwinged ears and a once-broken nose that had healed crookedly. His curly-brimmed straw hat supplied negligible shade, but after two weeks on a road gang, he was burned and browned past any concern for his hide.

His lips, though, were cracked and swollen, his eyes bloodshot and slitted against the silican glare they'd endured; the light gray-green of the irises were startling in the sun-blackened mask of his face. His hair was long and black, and matted with the same gray grit that powdered his thick brows and heavy beard stubble. His big-shouldered frame was almost massive; he would stand well over six

5

feet, muscled and unbent in a faded and sweat-salted shirt and Levi's with a number stenciled on the right thigh.

He touched his tongue to his cracked lips, looking longingly off toward the peaks that were beyond the white shimmer of desert to the south. Leedstock was down there. And Mexico; but Poe Lockhart's thoughts were fixed on this side of the border. *Leedstock*. It was frustrating as hell to know that a few more miles, relatively few in this vast country, on a straight course south would bring him to familiar ground, hills and woods and mountains, that were as familiar as the back of his hand. Where a man knew the springs and streams, where there was game to be snared, he could live off the land two weeks or three, as long as it took to get back his strength and lay his plans.

Instead he had let himself be trapped by his own insensate stubbornness. There were mountains to the east, west, and north of Coldrock Territorial Prison and the surrounding country; but Leedstock was to the south, and almost the whole distance to the Leedstock country was taken up by barren, open desert—no cover, practically no water, no shelter from the broiling sun, and leaving a trail that any good tracker could cinch.

A short swing to either side after his escape would have taken him into hospitable terrain where he could have shaken pursuit, rested up, then worked down to Leedstock by degrees along a slow, circuitous route. What the hell, after six years, had been all his hurry? Facing a crushing failure of his plans because of one piece of bad judgment, Poe let his lips twitch in a parched grin.

He was still calm, that was something, but the numb, fraying pace had pushed him, mind and body, to the end of his tether. He'd been running ahead of Rydell for a day and a night. His hands and feet were cut to ribbons, his shoes torn to shreds by young cacti and sharp rocks. He had not eaten in almost twenty-four hours; he had slaked his thirst once, at a slime-covered seep a mile or so back. Just possibly, the numb exhaustion in every fiber of his being was an advantage; he could no longer feel very much. Not being an Apache, he had been forging along on determination alone for some hours now and pain, if he felt it, could break down a man's drive sooner than tiring.

All the same, he was on his last legs, and now Rydell,

6

having finished his unhurried study of the facing slope, was starting up it on foot, leaving his horse. The escarpment was stony and treacherous; a horse would hamper a man on the search, and it was clear to Rydell that, since his quarry could be laid up behind any of fifty gigantic boulders up there, he could not be too careful.

Poe couldn't do a thing but remain motionless where he was, flattened like a leech along the ground, almost hugging the rounded boulder but not quite touching; the rock was sunraw and blazing hot.

No matter how it went now, he was bound to be discovered. Rydell was coming zigzag to cover this whole side of the promontory, peering around, his rifle swinging back and forth with his glance.

Poe was calm, but he had to tight-rein the idea of making a break. To run from a man with a horse and a rifle on open terrain would be to give way to a suicidal panic, and nothing more. He could grin because that was the way he was, but it didn't change his determination not to be returned to Coldrock.

Once he was back inside those high walls, the chance for which he had watched and waited would be gone forever. The prison officials would take no more chances with him. Setting up this chance alone had cost him an eternity of grinding patience and docile, even meek behavior that went against his grain.

A man considering escape from Coldrock had needed to take into his considerings the Gatling gun mounted above the main gate, the bounty trackers that would be set on his trail armed and provisioned, the miles of wilderness he would have to face afoot and barehanded. And, of course, the Snake Den, that desolate, fetid dungeon where he'd be imprisoned for a month or so, chained to the stone floor if he were brought back alive.

Poe's patience had paid off when the government decided to build a road through some rugged country and save costs by using convict labor. He supposed it was his record for tractable behavior that had caused him to be included in the group of convicts taken one morning from their cells and conveyed by wagon ten miles east to an old cavalry station, abandoned for seven years since the last hostiles had been put down. The convicts slept in the old troop barracks,

7

locked and barred and well guarded; they took their meals in the old mess hall under the eyes of watchful guards. Each morning they were taken by wagon to the site of operations. The convicts sat unchained in the wagon bed, but a hard-faced guard rode alongside, a Winchester across his pommel.

Poe had sized things with care before making his move. Every morning and night, coming and going, he studied the badly rutted trail the wagon followed. At one point the rough grade clung to a slope which sheered off on one side into a steep bare slope for about thirty feet. Below that was a tangle of brush and scrub pine extending to the base of the slope. The country beyond broke into a maze of ridges and canyons. A man could lose himself there for at least a short time till the trackers were set after him. If he made his break just before dark, he would give himself another edge.

The guard was alert and careful that first week; Poe waited for him to nod from the absence of trouble. When his vigilance started to relax, Poe was ready. One evening as they returned to the station, Poe left the wagon at the spot of his choice. He simply dived over the side, hit the slope rolling, and plunged downward into the scrub. He got his feet under him and fought through the clogging brush to the bottom, the guard's .45-70 slugs searching blindly for him in the growing twilight. Poe clung to thinning cover till he reached the first canyons, then laid low. There could be no pursuit till morning. When moonrise gave him some detail, he felt his way out of the canyons inside an hour.

He struck roughly south, wanting to cover as much ground as possible while darkness held. He was heading on a straight line for Leedstock County and familiar ground, and this had been the single blunder that had undone his whole escape. He did not know, he had only guessed at, the character of the country that lay between his point of escape and his destination. It was a nightmarish terrain, scorched and broken, enough to crack even his hardrock stamina.

Next day by mid-morning, he was stumbling with exhaustion. His body was punished by the savage sun, his shoes worn nearly through; he was beginning to suffer from lack of water. After getting a glimpse of his one pursuer from a ridgetop, Poe kept where possible to the roughest stretches, bitter for horse travel, but offering cover here and

8

there for a man afoot, also making tracking difficult. But he couldn't do much of this and hold to a straight course too; as his energy flagged, the man on his trail gained. Each time Poe checked the backtrail from cover, he was a little nearer. When the tracker got close enough to spot his quarry, it would be over; then he would simply ride his man down.

Poe had gotten halfway up the flinty face of the promontory when, finding himself ready to drop, he had dug in behind the boulder. He had played out his string, and all he could do was wait for the inevitable.

It all chased through his mind in a few weary seconds as he watched Rydell's stocky form toil up the slope, plodding heavily in his slow zigzag, poking from rock to rock.

He saw Rydell's line of ascent was carrying him well to the left of Poe's sheltering boulder, and instinctively now, Poe inched in a curving crawl on his belly around the rock, keeping it always between him and the tracker. Not that it really mattered; Rydell would cover the promontory back and forth, up and down, like a cruising hawk, till he found his man or some sign that could be followed.

Flattened motionless to the earth, his tattered and dust-soiled clothes blending into it, Poe followed Rydell by ear now to the summit, hearing him drop down along the other side.

Poe blinked—his brains must be stewed from the heat not to have thought of it instantly. Rydell's horse was ground-tied at the slope's base no more than a hundred yards below, and Rydell, for the moment, was cut off from view of both the horse and Poe's position.

Poe squinted through the shimmer of baked earth at the animal, a handsome, well-mettled brute, all rippling muscles and a shining bay coat under a dull caking of dust. He guessed the horse had plenty left in him, and there was a canteen of water on the saddle; there would be provisions in the bags and maybe a spare pistol. Poe's heart thudded against the earth.

Ready to risk all on a quick dash to reach the animal, he restrained himself. *If you run at him, maybe he'll spook.* Poe held in, straining his ears, but couldn't hear Rydell any longer. He didn't know how near or far the tracker might be now or exactly what he was up to; that was something to worry about, but it couldn't stop him.

Bracing his palms against the gritty earth, he started to shove onto his feet. A wave of weakness darkened his mind, and he thought he was going to faint. When he shut his eyelids, white sparks flailed behind them. He shuddered, knotting his hands in the ground, fighting back. *No more— no more. Fight it. Have to reach the horse.*

Carefully he pushed to his feet and moved downward hunched over deeply, his hands out on the air, ready to catch himself if he fell. The raw pain knifing up his legs from his feet made each step a rhythmic agony, but it had the effect of shocking him to full consciousness. His strides gained a lunging, awkward haste, and almost before he knew it, the horse was a few yards away.

Careful. Easy does it, boy. Putting down the driving urgency in him, he approached the animal carefully, quietly talking. The bay, not impressed, flattened his ears and sidled away. Poe followed him step by step, eyes on the trailing reins. A little nearer, just a little, and he'd dare to try for them.

A shout drifted down to him—Rydell was coming back and Poe was seen, and now he had to move, and fast. He grabbed wildly for the reins and missed as the horse leaped away, snorting.

Poe turned his head, his eyes narrowed with a red throbbing; Rydell was coming down the slope as fast as his stocky legs would carry him, shouting for Poe not to move again. *The hell with him.*

Pivoting, he started away toward the south at a painful trot, glancing back across his shoulder. Rydell had hauled up, and he began firing. The bullets screamed off the rocks to his right and left, and he knew Rydell was not shooting to kill. At any moment he might, but Poe swung on at his furious, excruciating trot.

He felt his legs caving, but he hung on blindly, still running after a fashion even as his feet flailed away his footing. He plunged face first into a fringe of young mesquite, skinning his face and hands some more. Rydell sent a bullet into the ground two feet from his head, and put another so close to his leg he felt the sting of dirt through his Levi's.

"Quit it," Rydell was yelling angrily. "Quit it, Poe! I'll bust you. I'll bust you cold right where you are, by God!"

A vast and fathomless disgust welled in Poe as he lay

10

there with his face against the dirt. For at least one minute escape had looked like a near thing—so near that another man might scream or curse. He did neither, but a dead weight of hopelessness was in his belly now. An ant crawled across the back of his hand; he shook it off, thinking wearily, *The hell with it,* and climbed slowly to his feet to wait for Rydell.

The tracker came laboriously down the slope. His stocky body was saddle-cramped enough to give him a kind of seaman's rolling gait as he came up, halting a few yards away. "Figure it was worth it, Poe? What did it get you?"

Poe let his shoulders lift and settle. "The Snake Den, I reckon."

Rydell shook his head, a square-built and solid man in a baggy black suit that was dusty and wrinkled. He had an honest, ruddy-brown face whose square lines gave him a deceptive look of bland contentment.

"A fool gaddamn thing, all right. You had only four more years, and I hazard they might of knocked some off that. You made a good record at Coldrock. You'll get another ten to twenty for this business. You might of made some chance for yourself if you had struck out east or west, even north. But south, even if you could of made it across the desert, a good tracker was bound to overhaul you on this kind of ground. With no horse or gun—Jesus, man. Must of wanted to get back to your old stamping grounds so bad you couldn't think straight."

"You think so, Tom?" Poe's tone was lean and unreadable.

Rydell gently curled his lips around a cold, damp, omnipresent cigar; he motioned with the rifle. "Let's be going."

11

CHAPTER TWO

Poe lay on his back in the scanty shade, eyes shut, letting the quivering red haze behind his eyelids cool back to a tolerable pink. He said, "When you quit being a deputy federal marshal, Tom?"

Rydell chuckled. "When I got a job heading up the Pima trackers for Coldrock for a sight more pay. When I had the word you'd escaped, I set out on your trail without the Pimas. I helped bring you in six years ago, and it seemed kind of a personal thing to bring you back on my own."

"And not very hard, seeing you was after a man with no gun or horse."

"Surest thing you know," Rydell said cheerfully.

Rydell had backtracked with his prisoner across the hot flats perhaps a mile; they were nooning in the dry creek bed where Poe had stumbled on a slimy waterhole in his flight. A scrub growth of cottonwoods and sycamores gave a thin cheer of greenery to the place. While Poe was resting, Rydell had watered his horse; he'd gathered dead brush and built a fire.

Now Poe strained his eyes open; he watched Rydell fill a pan with murky water and set it on the fire. He whistled all the while and seemed not to watch his prisoner, but Poe knew he was watching every minute and not even thinking about it.

When the water was bubbling, Rydell took it off the flames and set it at Poe's side, and got out a pint of whiskey and some clean rags that had been a shirt once. "Soon's that water's cool, clean out them cuts. Put on some of that Irish milk too and tie up the worst."

Poe sat up and gingerly worked off his shredded shoes. During the trek, the soles had largely parted company with the insteps, still flapping loosely after he had anchored them with strips torn from his shirt. His feet were in ugly shape, savagely lacerated by sharp rocks and cactus spines. Poe

12

washed them and doused them liberally with a raw fury of whisky. Afterward he took a long, luxurious pull at the bottle, his first drink in six years, before tying up the open cuts and blisters. His palms had suffered little less than his feet, but he bound only light strips around the heels of his hands. He wanted them unhampered by clumsy rags, free for action, if opportunity offered. Not soon though, not with a broiled weariness pulling at his body, and his thoughts soggy and slow-budging.

Rydell dug out hardtack and jerky and gave Poe some, and set his canteen where Poe could reach it. Afterward Rydell took the shabby cigar from his teeth and tucked it carefully away in his coat; he ate standing up, the rifle under his arm.

Poe half-lidded his gray-green eyes. "What happened to McKelvey? Still a U. S. marshal?"

"Unh-unh. Government retired him. Sixty-six last spring, but you'd never know it. Think a man would slow down, but not Mac. He stewed and cussed the government a spell, then went to the Parkinson Detective Agency and asked for a job. They was glad to get a man with his knowledge of this territory, and now he heads the agency's whole operation here."

Poe wasn't surprised, remembering that long ride north with McKelvey and Rydell six years ago. A prisoner could pass talk, even josh about his predicament, with the amiable Rydell. There was no fun about the white-haired, granite-visaged McKelvey; he'd been all duty and dedication.

Poe ate slowly, his thoughts moving back far beyond that night and his capture by McKelvey. He thought of Emmaline and his two sons, and of Ben Yarbrough; and there his thoughts halted and jelled with a silent ferocity.

He and Ben had first met twenty-four years ago on some forgotten ranch job; Poe could recall only that it had been a natural friendship from the first. Orphans both, they had been a pair of youthful catamounts who had bunked and boarded together, "seen the elephant" together, and pulled up stakes together whenever the time seemed ripe to drift.

They had gone together to the Saturday night dance in Leedstock where they first met Emmaline Fancher. Leedstock County was more noted for its mines than its ranches, and most of the mining interests were owned by

Barrett Fancher; but neither Poe nor Ben were aware when they began sparking her that Emmaline was his daughter, just returned from finishing school.

That she would inherit considerable wealth meant very little to Emmaline; it had meant nothing at all to Poe Lockhart, which had impressed her favorably. Ben, on the other hand, had been overwhelmed by the idea of courting an heiress. Both youths had known intense poverty, but their reactions to the experience had been opposite. Because Poe, who could never take very much seriously, had learned that he could get along on next to nothing, money had meant too little to him. To Ben, the ambitious one, loathing the memory of a deprived boyhood, money had meant too much. Yet Poe had never had cause to doubt that Ben, as much as he, had loved Emmaline.

At first it had been a half-game with the two of them, like much of the rough-and-tumble rivalry that seasoned their friendship. For awhile, as the contest grew more determined, only the good humor of the two rivals suffered; but as time went along, a real and ominous sharpness had developed. And after Emmaline made her choice, things were never again the same between them.

Though Yarbrough had taken the blow with his head up, it became increasingly apparent over the years, as he never married, as he paid frequent visits to the Lockharts, becoming a second father to their two boys, how deeply losing Emmaline had affected him.

Though Poe and Ben had each developed his own ranch from a shoestring beginning, Yarbrough enjoyed a middling success, while Poe was beset by one reversal after another. This fact did nothing to relieve the strain. Life had settled into a grinding struggle for the Lockhart family.

Even after Emmaline's health had gone bad, she'd taken every setback in calm stride, doing the best she could with what they had, never complaining, calmly turning down her father's offers of money because of the dry, wicked satisfaction in his manner when he made them. Barrett Fancher—that small, dapper, cigar-puffing man with the manner of an indignant gamecock who had never understood how it was that a cow-country ruffian with little education and few courtesies had dared to court and marry

14

Emmaline, nor how his pretty, serious, iron-willed daughter could ignore his wishes in the matter. Poe's steady failures had let Fancher feel vindicated in his first indictment of Emmaline's husband as a ne'er-do-well with no teeth in his good intentions.

In a few short years, Poe had lost the gift for words and laughter. That the taciturn gloom cloaking the Lockhart household was relieved only by Ben's visits had increased his morose broodings. And, though this may have been resentful fancy, it had seemed to Poe that Yarbrough went consistently out of his way to point up his success and Poe's failure, dressing in the latest cut and style, coming to visit in a fancy buggy with matched bays, never neglecting the boys' birthdays, bringing gifts every Christmas.

When a man had an unbridled streak to begin with, nothing was needed but a prodding of blind circumstance to drive him in anger down a different forking. A shared restlessness in their characters had once made Poe and Ben closer than brothers, but Ben had successfully channeled his tendency into ambition that was fed by hard work and luck and the sense of responsibility that grows with a man's material possessions. Poe's untamed streak had been cooled down by marriage and home, only to flare back with a bitter-fresh sting as time went along, when everything he put his hand to soured.

First the penny ante brand-blotting, furtively and alone; then taking up with a handful of other ne'er-do-wells for a bit of larger-scale rustling, the quick strikes, the short night drives, the hidden hide-and-tallow plant in the hills. It was the kind of crookedness a man could swallow and pat his belly on because he felt sorry for himself and knew he deserved something more and because, all told, it was hard work. He found the others looking more and more to him for leadership. A prospering ranch, a buggy and bays, spit 'n' polish wasn't necessary to capture their respect; a quick gun and a hard fist would do it.

Then the sheriff's ambush, discovery, death for some, capture for others. Poe, escaping with a few others, had led them into the rugged mountain country east of Leedstock, where an army could lose itself without trying. *All right, you bastards,* he had silently told the valleyed town and people

15

and society he couldn't live with. *You all got yours, you smug bastards, and you're going to give me mine, like it or not. You want war, war it'll be.*

Poe had known those peaks well; he made them his base of operations, moving about as frequently as whim or caution dictated, locating his quick break-up camps in every place from caves to deserted mining camps. He had made his strikes both faraway and close to home, from train robbery and bank holdups to horse-thieving and cattle-rustling, selling the stolen stock of many brands by showing well-forged bills of sale to his buyers in various places.

The range of his activities had seemed random and patternless, but this aspect was as deliberate as the planning of each job. Baffled lawmen thought that most of his actions were based on convenience or caprice, and that was what Poe had wanted them to think. He knew that no matter how well each individual job went, the day that some astute sheriff or marshal found a pattern in his methods and anticipated him would be the day before the finish.

He had carefully avoided any action that might hurt his wealthy father-in-law and upset the strange and delicate relationship Poe still had with Emmaline and his sons. She, a frail and sickly woman, had maintained standards like iron. To Emmaline, her loyalty to her marriage vow meant that she must never betray her husband by word or act, also that he had every right—as the father of her sons—to see the boys when he chose. By the same stern token, her disapproval of him was total. She took care to counteract any effect of his on the two boys by a rigid moral training. Poe, in his turn, respected this training, giving his sons distinct hints that they would damned well be good and God-fearing if that was what their mother wanted.

By their adolescent years, a divided influence had shaped each boy in his own specific mold. Wyatt, the older one, quiet and serious, took after his mother. He could never quite conceal the fear and distaste his father was gradually inspiring in him. Gilbert, on the other hand—partly because he was younger but mostly because he was his father's image inside and out—lived for his father's unexpected visits.

For taking no chances, Poe made his visits to his ranch infrequent and irregular, coming only after dark and reconnoitering the place with care before slipping into the house.

Their support was a problem, for Emmaline would not accept a cent of stolen money. Hence it was Ben Yarbrough who provided what they needed, Emmaline taking his money reluctantly and insisting, in her stiff aversion to charity, that she visit Ben's ranch two days every week to tidy his bachelor house. Knowing Emmaline, Poe understood that was all there was to the visits, though in the nature of things she and Ben were bound to become closer.

About the time his depredations had become bold and far-flung enough to cause a public clamor, a new United States marshal, a man seasoned in Western ways, was assigned to the territory. Bart McKelvey had been following the situation for some time before it was dropped in his arms; he'd made his plans at once and followed them up as quickly. He and his deputy, Tom Rydell, had gone into Leedstock County incognito, as drummers selling newfangled equipment for ranch and farm. The two of them had ingratiated themselves with the natives and unearthed a piece of information here, a piece there.

Poe could not know about McKelvey, but considering all the public uproar, things had gotten suspiciously quiet. He became careful; he scaled down all his activities and also decided that, with all his precautions, he could no longer be sure of visiting his family in safety.

Ben Yarbrough, still playing the loyal and generous friend, had suggested that since the law might post a watch on the Lockhart home, Poe could see his sons at Ben's place. Emmaline could bring the boys along now and then on the days when she came to clean, letting it look like a casual visit. Now and then too, they might find it convenient to stay overnight at Ben's. Poe could drift in after dark to visit them.

Of course, as Yarbrough pointed out, this would make necessary their knowing exactly when Poe planned each visit; but since the information wouldn't go beyond Emmaline and himself, for even Ben's ranchhands would be kept ignorant, there would really be no extra risk involved. For all the coolness that had grown up between them, Poe had no reason not to trust Ben Yarbrough. Once they had been closer than brothers, and Poe knew his man: there was no treachery in Ben, he thought.

On his first visit, Poe proceeded as they had agreed, ground-tying his horse a fair distance from Ben's house so as not to alert the crew. Then he worked in on foot through the darkness. He reached Ben's back door and opened it. And found himself looking squarely into the muzzle of Bart McKelvey's pistol.

Apparently there was nobody else about, but Poe never had time to find out. McKelvey wasted no words at all; he had simply slapped the cuffs on Poe's hands, and inside of ten minutes was jogging north with his prisoner. Toward dawn they halted by a stream, where Rydell rendezvoused with them. By early morning the three of them were out of Leedstock County, and Poe had not seen Ben Yarbrough again, nor Emmaline, nor his sons.

A good attorney had gotten almost all of the many charges brought against him thrown out for lack of evidence; yet the indictments that had stuck were enough to net him ten to twenty years in the Territorial Prison at Coldrock. . . .

Rydell cracked the bleak train of Poe's thoughts, saying phlegmatically, "Time to be moving." Rydell restored the cigar to his mouth, then fetched a pair of worn moccasins from his saddlebag and tossed them to Poe. "I use these for foot tracking sometimes. You got a couple coal scuttles for feet, but try 'em anyway."

Shortly, they were heading north again, Poe moving ahead on foot, Rydell idling along an easy eight yards behind him on horseback. Despite the shabby comfort of the moccasins, Poe's feet made a steady misery. Rydell did not press a hard pace; Poe was grateful for that, and he felt no malice about their respective positions. No need for Rydell to explain that he would not permit Poe to ride because he was fully aware that once Poe got a horse under him, he would try a break.

Since Rydell wasn't returning Poe to the old cavalry station close to where he'd made his break, but directly back to the main prison miles to the west, he chose a more westerly route back, a north-northwest angle as Poe figured it. They were crossing the same desert area and the heat and monotony were the same; only Poe's mood differed.

Before, he'd been the running quarry, but he had run with a hope. By early tomorrow, he would be back inside

18

Coldrock, facing an increased sentence and a tightened security—after a month or so of confinement in the fetid, perpetual night of the Snake Den. The privilege he had built up as a model jailbird would be wiped out; there would be no more outside work for an untrustworthy prisoner.

Somewhere, somehow, before they reached Coldrock he had to find a last-ditch chance for escape. It narrowed down in his mind this tightly—*make it or die*—and now a quiet and wicked determination hardened in him.

CHAPTER THREE

As the morning wore on, they started to climb off the sun-blistered flats. The scrub desert character of the land didn't change, but the country was more rugged and broken. Poe soon found that Rydell knew no more about this stretch than he himself; nothing. He realized as much when, after traversing a canyon floor for a half mile, they came to a box end that was unscalable. They had to backtrack until they could leave the canyon and make a detour still farther west.

The land heightened steadily as they pushed on, but the heights ended quite abruptly at a sharp dropaway. A massive east-west running fault that had convulsed itself out of the desert floor in a bygone age made a nearly sheer drop for a couple hundred feet. They could work along the rim east or west to where the cliff tapered off, or make an attempt to descend here.

Deadpan, Rydell inspected the situation, then told Poe to walk ahead of him westerly along the rim. Poe did, while Rydell, following behind, paid strict attention to the cliff below.

They came to a dim trail that led off the rim down the wall at a rather steep angle, bending out and in along each irregularity and indentation. Though the trail had apparently scaled and faulted out of the wall, it looked as if Indian hands had been at work at some time or other, chipping away with flints to make the descent more negotiable.

Rydell called a rest halt before tackling the trail down. He dismounted and tucked his cigar away, and built himself a smoke, setting the makings and a match where Poe could reach them. Squatting on the rimrock, Poe rolled a cigarette between his work-thickened fingers and studied the dropoff. Beyond it, the land pancaked into a shimmering plain, making easy going probably clear to Coldrock. He looked at the trail. The scale appeared loose and treacherous; a man would have to watch his step all the way to the bottom, and there were places a wide-barreled horse might never get past. He was reflecting that any trick he tried to turn while on this trail would pose as much danger to him as it would to Rydell. "Let's go," said the tracker.

Poe spoke for the first time in hours. "Bad place for a horse."

"Bad enough. He's like to make trouble." Rydell considered for a moment. "All right, you take the reins and lead him down. If he balks, I'll be behind to hooraw him along."

Rydell pulled his pistol and stepped away from his horse before motioning Poe to pick up the reins. Poe did, then led off down the trail, picking his way carefully. Here and there the surface was soft and dangerous from recent slides; scale went rattling down the cliff every time he planted his foot. The soft footing made the horse increasingly skittish; Poe had to tug him onward in a half-dozen places, talking low all the while. He could have cursed his frustration; he was getting no chance at all. Moving the horse along was demanding his full attention while Rydell, taking no chances here, kept his pistol out and a watchful eye on Poe.

Poe curled his lip stiffly around his cigarette, using both hands to maneuver the horse past yet another bad place. He saw that ahead, the going would be still worse; the trail curved too sharply around an abutting angle of rock. He called back, "Don't know as we can make it here."

"We'll make it. Keep pulling him along."

Poe drew on the fraction of cigarette still clamped in his teeth; the hot smoke scorched his tongue and he raised a hand to toss the butt away, then dropped the hand back to the reins. *Wait a minute. Maybe.*

20

The bay's left flank began to scrape the wall; the horse went stiff-legged and rolled his eyes, shying back. Poe tugged and Rydell hoorawed from behind. The horse took a few more steps and then, as the trail pinched down farther, he panicked. In his fright he tried to quarter back on Rydell. The trail here was too narrow for turning; he would go over and drag Poe with him if Poe held on.

Poe caught the headstall and swung his weight backward to pull the bay's swinging head around. "Hold him!" Rydell shouted.

"Never make it down," Poe said. The animal was snorting and trembling, but Poe's hold on his head steadied him somewhat. "Have to turn back, Tom. Find another way to the bottom."

Rydell swore softly. "All right." He rammed his pistol into its holster, then edged up by the horse's haunch and took hold of the saddle. "I'll steady him on the outside and you try to back him up."

Slowly, step by step, pulling and talking quietly, they crowded the bay backward. As the trail safely widened, Rydell said, "We'll turn him here. Hold that headstall tight."

Poe drew on his fragment of cigarette, then cursed as if he'd burned his lips and quickly brought a hand to the butt to snatch it from his mouth. In almost the same motion he stabbed the glowing tip into the horse's neck just ahead of the left forehock with a hard, grinding twist. At the same time he let go of the reins and headstall.

The bay squealed in pain and terror, wheeling sideways and outward. Poe had gambled that he'd shy oppositely from the source of the pain; he did. His front legs plunged off the rim at the same instant his shoulder smashed Rydell in the chest.

Rydell took a step back, straining for balance, his body arched and poised on the trail's edge. Then he was overbalanced, his hands clawing at the air. Poe had a blurred impression of his broad face, stupefied with surprise, his mouth open. And he was gone.

The bay's front hoofs were over, but his superb musculature saved him; he reacted like chain lightning, rearing his rump backward and crumpling his hindquarters. Most of his weight stayed on the ledge, and then Poe was at

21

his side hauling at the reins. The bay struck at the crumbling rim with his forefeet, his shoes ringing; one hoof took hold on the rough rock, and he pushed back onto his feet with a strong assist from Poe.

He held the animal tightly, speaking, stroking his muzzle, till his quivering stopped. Then, holding the reins loosely, Poe stepped to the edge of the trail and looked down. The boiling dust was still settling from Rydell's plunge down the near-vertical slant. The tracker was down there on his back, his thick body twisted across a heavy boulder with a kind of impossible grotesquery. Poe's throat tightened; he thought, *I didn't want this,* but then he was not sure. They had gotten most of the way to the bottom, and maybe Rydell was only knocked out.

Poe left the horse, anchoring the reins to a heavy chunk of roc'-, and scrambled heedlessly down the trail to the base of the cliff. He stopped by Rydell's sprawled form. The tracker looked as if he had gone to sleep, but then Poe saw for the first time how his gray head rested against a rock. Gently he turned the head. First his hand touched something wet and slick, and he saw the matted wet darkness of the hair. He felt for a pulse and then a heartbeat.

Poe rocked back on his heels, arms slung over his knees, tasting the bitter fullness of his victory. *I didn't want this, but who'll believe it?* But then it didn't really matter.

He hadn't meant to knock Rydell clear off the trail, nor to kill him. The fact remained that a constituted official had been killed by a fugitive, a desperate man, and that made all the difference. When a man on the wrong side of the law killed without witnesses, whether intentionally or not, he was a killer.

Maybe in his desperation he would have killed anyway, deliberately, had there been no alternative; but somehow he had never considered that he would have to. By a stroke of blind luck nobody had been killed by his gang during his years of outlawry. But Poe had never considered it luck. For all his name with a gun, he had never shot to kill; he'd always warned his men to follow his example. He had simply reasoned, always, that killing had no part in his scheme of outlawry, and that was all there was to it. Now, quite suddenly, his careless luck had run out. He was a

22

killer, and he knew at first hand a feeling he'd never had to face.

The hell with that too. Killer or not, he had made a resolution never to see the inside of another prison cell, and that applied whether the law came after him for murder or for spitting on a sidewalk. He was free now, really free by God, and any man who took him again would have to take him face down—never alive. He was sorry about Rydell, but his quick hard fatalism did not linger with that thought. The thing was done.

Reaching out, he yanked the tracker's pistol from the holster and felt the old surge of confidence that the feel of a good gun against his palm brought. He had a pistol now and a saddle gun; he had a sound horse, some grub, and a little water. Enough to get him where he wanted to go, and he knew where he was going exactly. The harsh lines around Poe's mouth tightened; he raised Rydell's body enough to strip off the coat.

CHAPTER FOUR

Poe buried Rydell's body in the stony ground not far from where he had fallen, afterward taking pains to erase every mark of what had happened. The prison officials would do some guessing when Rydell failed to return, but could have no way of substantiating their guesses. Meantime he would have to get rid of Rydell's clothes as soon as possible. Far too stolid to be bothered by wearing a coat and trousers taken from a man he had killed accidentally, he yet found the suit a pure misery after the ragged comfort of his giveaway prison clothes. His big-muscled body strained every seam; the sleeves and legs were too short by inches.

Traveling by night only, Poe quickly reached the familiar hills and woods of Leedstock County. He found a cave that he knew of, and laid up for two days and nights to recuperate. In that time, he got back most of his strength; his hands and feet were still tender, but once he was sure they'd escaped infection, he gave them no more thought: he had things to do.

On the third morning, as the rising sun made a flat bloodwelt of light on the horizon, he topped a rocky crest above the broad rolling basin that held Leedstock. From here he had a panoramic view: the serpentine crawl of the Blue River twisting down to the lower basin where the town sprawled; and over toward this end the buildings of Talon, Ben Yarbrough's ranch, were plainly visible. Poe's eyes smoldered; his hand gripped his saddle pommel till the veins stood out. The old question burned like a branding iron in his mind.

He was still sure that Emmaline had taken no willing part in the trap that had been sprung on him that night six years ago at good old Ben's ranch. Emmaline's attitude toward him had become almost impersonal; he was an irritant she had accepted because of a firm conviction of his parental rights. In a brief letter, she had told him she'd known nothing about a plan to capture him until Mr. Rydell had shown up at the Lockhart place the day they were to visit Ben's. Rydell had told her nothing except that he was a U.S. deputy marshal, but had confined the boys and her to their home all that day and night. He was firm and very polite, and had left before dawn with no word of explanation.

Later, learning of Poe's capture, she had queried Ben, who could tell her only that McKelvey had come to his place about the same time Rydell was visiting hers, and had taken him into town and turned him over to the sheriff, who had agreed not to release him till next morning; then McKelvey had left. Ben had no more idea than she who had tipped off McKelvey. She intended, Emmaline had added in closing, to raise her sons to the best of her ability. That was all; that was her explanation and her goodbye to Poe and what he represented, and respecting her unspoken wish, he had written no reply.

Emmaline was far too tight-scrupled to betray the man she had taken for better or worse, nor would she lie. That left Yarbrough, and Poe had figured it out carefully. McKelvey would have no difficulty learning that Ben Yarbrough had once been his closest frined, but that the relation had cooled. Feeling out the possibilities, McKelvey would go to Ben. What arguments he had given Ben or by

24

what rationale Ben had arrived at the noble conclusion that it was his duty to rid Emmaline of a renegade husband wasn't important. Treachery had never been a quality of Ben's, but any man could bend a scruple to breaking if something he desired enough were at stake: in this case, Emmaline.

Within six months after Poe's conviction, she had obtained a divorce; in less than another half-year she was Mrs. Ben Yarbrough. Ben had kept him faithfully posted on everything: the birth of a son, Ben Junior, and the steady weakening of Emmaline's health afterward. One night a little over two years ago, she had died quietly in her sleep. When Ben had informed him, Poe had felt almost nothing on his account; it was Ben's grief, barbed and bitter, that Poe had felt behind each scrawled word.

There could be no doubting the intensity of Ben's loss of a woman he had always loved but had won for only a brief, wrenching time. Nor in any of his letters to Poe had there been a note of gloating or triumph; they were friendly and matter-of-fact letters, dwelling with considerate brevity on everything except news of Poe's two sons for which he was always hungry, and here Ben had gone into a welcome detail. It had been a decent enough gesture on Ben's part, but a cheap one, and no more than a thin sop for his conscience, Poe had guessed. He was tempted to ride down now and confront Ben, but that meeting had been postponed for six years; it could wait a little longer.

For it wasn't the prospect of looking up Ben Yarbrough that had triggered Poe's decision to break out of Coldrock at once, rather than serve the four remaining years of his sentence. It was Ben's letter of a month ago that had changed everything. After that letter, waiting out these few weeks for a chance at escape had driven Poe almost beyond endurance.

Ben had first mentioned the wild streak becoming apparent in Poe's son Gilbert two years ago, just after Emmaline had died. Gil was eighteen and feeling his oats, and his mother's death had made an upset, that was all, Ben had assured Poe. But as time went along the wildness developed to a cut of downright mean, and in Ben's letter of a month back, he'd told of how Gil had prodded one of the Talon crew into a fight and shot the man in the arm and leg,

25

crippling him for life. Then Gil had disappeared. A week or so later Ben learned that Gil had been seen with Clem Dundie's gang of wild ones.

Dundie had been Poe's outlaw lieutenant; after Poe was captured, Dundie and some others had headed for Mexico. Poe knew that the governor had declared a general amnesty for all his men, judging that without Poe to hold them together most of them would need only a little encouragement to quit the outlaw's game. So there had been nothing to prevent Dundie from returning to his old haunts north of the border. Now he and a tough crew had taken over a deserted mountain town called Jenny Camp, where Dundie was lording it like a gypsy king. He was also suspected of robbing some bullion trains, though nobody could prove it.

And Gil had taken up with Dundie's gang.

From the day his older son, Wyatt, was born, Poe had taken a deep and genuine pride in his fatherhood and had always done as conscientiously by his boys as circumstances had allowed. When they were small, both Wye and Gil had worshipped him. His sons had been a single bright spot in those trying days when he was still a struggling shoestring rancher and Emmaline's ironlike Puritanism, deepening over the years, had gradually come like a wall between them.

Later, when an outlaw's career had made any normal relation with them impossible, he had done his best to counter the miserable example he was setting. But he'd long since come to the bitter knowledge that the best thing he could have done in that regard was to stay completely away from his sons rather than press contacts that had set one son against him and caused the other to idolize all that was wrong in him. Poe was the kind of man who could ignore all judgments but his own—no matter how you cut it, the responsibility had been his, and so had been the failure.

Poe had forged his own road in life; he was too irreligious for atonement, too unemotional for regret, and too independent to give a damn what anyone thought. But looking back at the bitter bed he had made for himself was reason enough for seeing to it that no son of his repeated his own mistakes.

Wyatt, loathing his father's memory, presented no such

26

problem as his brother; and Poe was too much of a loner and a fatalist to brood about Wye's opinion of him. What was done was done, and what couldn't be changed must be accepted. Ben Yarbrough had told him of Wye's graduation with honors from Harvard Law School and the excellent prospects his talent and ambition seemed to fit him for. In that regard, no father could ask for more; the main thing was that Wye was well and doing well. Wye was even welcome to his hatred of Poe if, as Poe guessed, it was a strong element in his making as a man.

But Gil, not yet hardened in his ways, could be changed by a father's determined will. *Hell, he's just wild,* Poe thought. *So was I at that age and I changed right enough. That wasn't what pushed me into outlawing. He's a kid and he's wild.*

It was with no hesitation now that Poe turned away from the basin, pulling his horse's head around toward the deep mountains . . . and Jenny Camp.

He rode steadily through the morning into heightening country, crossing high slopes cloaked by the cool green of vaulting conifers and checkered by meadows of thick grama grass. It irritated him that the area had changed enough during his years in prison to make crow's-flight travel impossible for a man who wanted to avoid being seen. He knew the hills, the flats, the streams, like his own hand; but the high ground, like the lowlands around Leedstock, was getting filled up with sheep and cattle outfits. Except when he was in the trees, he rarely missed the settlers' shacks—a flash of sunlight off a window or a thread of chimney smoke. It was still miles between neighbors, but always there was the risk of blundering into somebody or other, and caution flagged down his progress; he made numerous detours.

By mid-afternoon, he left the settled country behind, but sunset had crowned the peaks and faded into gray low dusk when he picked up the thin scatter of lights that was Jenny Camp. The town, typical of the deserted mining camps that dotted these mountains, was a makeshift community of bad masonry and worse carpentry thrown up some years ago by miners flocking in to stake claims on a flash strike. In less than a year, the strike had petered out and the camp had gone over to the packrats and termites. A few frame

27

buildings, a store and hotel and saloon and blacksmith shop, were still maintained for the trickle of trade offered by trappers, drifters, and various shady characters.

Aside from the further ravages of time, Jenny Camp hadn't changed a jot, Poe saw as he rode down the crooked trail of a street. The saloon was the place to get information and look for familiar faces. Poe dismounted by the sagging steps and tied his horse, and went in.

A suspended kerosene lamp made a smoky light and murky shadows in the small barroom. Three men were playing cards at a lone deal table; a couple more were drinking at the plank bar. All motion and talk drifted to a standstill as they watched him cross to the bar. Poe scanned their faces and didn't know a one, but he knew their stamp as well as any man alive. A complete stranger got a careful sizing-up because you could never be sure of anyone, stranger or not.

The bartender, a stocky towhead with hard humorous eyes and probably as spotty a backtrail as any man in the room, said in a rich Southern voice, "Hoddy. Drink?"

Poe rang a coin on the bar and looked around the room again. The players had picked up their game, but talk did not resume, and he knew they were half-waiting. If he had a quick drink and left, they would relax; the longer he remained, the more tension would thicken. He might as well ask his questions at once, but being too direct would get him nothing.

Swallowing his drink first, he said to the bartender, "Looking for a man. Maybe you know him. Red Mercy." Mercy, a member of his old gang, had been a gray, inconspicious man, all but unknown outside outlaw circles.

A chair scraped loudly; a glance across his shoulder told Poe it was one of the cardplayers getting up to come to the bar, and he looked back at the bartender. "You know him? Mercy?"

The cardplayer, moving against the bar just then, brushed Poe's coat and murmured, "Excuse me. Er, a whiskey, please, Alabam."

He was a youngish man, strongly built, with long ash-blond hair that brushed the quilted collar of his green frock coat. He wore fawn-colored trousers and a silk shirt with a string tie. His wide, mobile lips were clamped around a thin cigar, and he squinted blank-eyed against the furling smoke.

"Sho, Dandy Mack," the bartender said, and grinned at Poe. "Red Mercy, hunh? That's him over there." He nodded at one of the two players remaining at the table, a lean young redhead needing a shave.

Poe thought, *Not by twenty years and fifty pounds he's not,* a swift wariness touching him then.

The bartender had spoken loudly, and the other men in the room looked at him, then at each other. The red-haired youth at the table said, "I quit," and, throwing in his cards, got up and walked out. The ash-blond man said, "Oh, er, wait up there, Mercy," and swallowed his drink, then followed the redhead out the door.

Everybody was looking at Poe now. He took his drink and stared back and said, "Anybody know Clem Dundie?"

Nobody said a word. Poe signaled for a refill, downed that too, and slowly turned his back and tramped to the door. He halted, looking out across the batwings. Under the outstream of lamplight the street looked deserted, but he wondered. Pushing open the doors, he went out and swung right toward the store, intending to ask his questions there.

Before he had gone five steps, a gun opened up across the street. A bullet boomed into the dry boards of the building a yard or so ahead of him. He stopped. The shot had been meant to warn, not kill, but his bafflement was kindling into anger now.

Deliberately he pivoted, strode back to the tie rail where his horse was, and yanked his rifle from its scabbard. He hip-braced it and levered as fast as he could, pumping shots into the dark alley across the way where he had caught the gunflash. He heard the bullets hammer against the rotted walls, then a curse and a sound of running feet.

Somebody else shot from down the street, and there was a crack of splitting wood as a bullet ricochetted off the tie rail. This was no warning shot, and Poe knew the redhead and Dandy Mack had set it up to hooraw him out of town—but why? He thought grimly, *You did something wrong,* and wheeled and lunged for the blackness of the areaway adjoining the saloon, reaching it as the other men spilled out through the batwing doors.

Poe reached the alley's end and veered to his left across the weed-grown lot. Dimly he heard someone yell, "Around

29

back, Chuck," and feet come pounding up the areaway. He thought dismally, *You're in for it now,* knowing the whole town would be on his back in a minute. If only one man in the saloon had known him, this couldn't have happened.

At the far rear corner of the next building, Poe veered again, just as he heard the running men reach the back of the areaway. A confusion of voices was lifting as he swung back toward the street again. Someone was bawling for a lantern.

Poe swept the street with a glance. Momentarily there was nobody in sight, but to try to reach his horse and ride out would be to present a clean target till he was past the lights. Anyhow he had come to Jenny Camp to stay, not be chased out by a clumsy handful of unnerved men. What he had to do was locate somebody who knew him. There would be Dundie, if nobody else. And Gil. But where the hell were they? And why had Dandy Mack and the redhead set a deadfall for him?

A swift hunch came to him, and he stabbed a hand into his coat pocket. Rydell's bulky wallet with its identification papers, which he had retained for any possible use, was gone. Then he remembered how Dandy Mack had brushed against him in the bar. By now they'd all be assured that a man who was both a territorial prison official and an ex-U. S. deputy marshal was snooping about.

The realization gave a fresh edge to Poe's danger; somehow he had to avoid the searchers till he could find somebody to correct their misconception. *If you're seen now, you're dead for sure.*

CHAPTER FIVE

The voices of the angry men told him they were splitting apart to look everywhere, and a couple of them were moving around behind the building whose dark corner he was hugging. At the moment the street was still deserted, and there was no time to lose.

Poe broke away from the shadow and went across the

mud-churned avenue, running. He heard a shout and knew he was seen, and then he was darting through another alley and was cut off briefly. For an instant he hauled up in the utter blackness behind the buildings, angry at his ill luck. In a minute or so they would be covering this side of town, and with lanterns. The old buildings would offer no refuge, since they could search each in turn. His best chance was to push straight out from town into the brush and lay low there till things quieted down.

He took five steps and collided solidly with a wall. *What the hell?* In the darkness, running his hands over a rough wood surface, he found he had walked into a high board fence, probably an old enclosure for a yard or garden. He began fumbling his way along it, feeling with his hands for any sort of gap he could climb through.

". . . . saw him go in here." That was the redhead's voice, and Dandy Mack's answered it. The two of them were coming down the alley at a trot, and Poe heard a match struck and saw a sulphurous flare of light.

He had just time to melt to the ground by the fence, face down in the litter of cans and bottles and rank grass, as they came out of the alley into the yard. Poe's heart pounded against the earth; his pistol was in his hand. He only hoped the tall grasses would conceal his body from the shadowy flicker of matchlight. Dandy Mack swore quietly.

"Well, I seen him go this way," the redhead drawled. "Listen, didn't he remind you o' somebody?"

"Gil Lockhart," Dandy Mack said promptly. "A look alike means nothing, Chuck."

"Well, Alabam didn't fool him none calling me Red Mercy. You could tell."

"No, but a lawman could know Red's face. What a lawman *wouldn't* know was that Red was killed over a card fight in Sonora a year ago. Besides I've heard of this Rydell; he's a lawman all right, even if the papers I took off him hadn't told as much. You go on back and fetch a lantern. Can't tell a Goddamn thing for certain with a match. Damn!"

Dandy Mack dropped the match, apparently as it singed his fingers, and the light died quickly. Poe heard Chuck's footsteps retreat up the alley; Dandy Mack struck a second match. The watery shadows shifted as Dandy Mack began

31

to prowl the yard, moving along the back wall of the building. Through the grass stems, Poe caught a flameglint on the gun in the man's right hand—the match was palm-cupped in his left.

Where the fence met the wall, Dandy Mack made a right-angle turn and worked slowly outward along the enclosure. In a few seconds, Poe knew, he would be seen. Pressed flat in the grass, he tensed his fist around the gun. And then a breath of wind blew out the match.

Even as Dandy Mack's brittle curse came, Poe was rising silently out of the grass. He saw the lines of Dandy's Macky's head and shoulders and that was all he needed as he moved in, gun raised. A startled grunt left Dandy Mack; he was aware of Poe's nearness then, but too late.

Poe swung his gun in a stiff arc, slashing the barrel savagely across Dandy Mack's jaw. The meeting of steel and bone made an ugly, flesh-muffled sound—the man went down without a whisper.

Swiftly, Poe searched the unconscious gambler's pockets, identified his stolen wallet by feel, and appropriated it. By matchlight he had seen there was no break in the seven-foot fence, and it looked too sturdy to kick his way through. He couldn't return to the street, and that left only one way.

He had noticed in the match's flare that the building had a back door. Leaving his bulky rifle in the grass, he felt his way to it and tripped the latch and went in, shutting the door again. He was in a black room with a musty odor of stored goods, and he saw next to the floor a pencil of light that meant a door with a lighted room beyond. Things had been happening too quickly for him to take his bearings; now he realized he was in a storeroom at the rear of the hotel.

Poe tiptoed to the door and eased it open a crack. The lobby, dimly illumined by the desk lamp, was deserted. The clerk, if there were a clerk, must have been pulled outside by the ruckus. Crossing the lobby, he went up the rickety stairs. At the head of the stairwell, another lamp shabbily lighted a corridor and the unnumbered doors on either side.

Poe halted, listening, mildly puzzled at the mutter of underpitched voices from several of the rooms. Quite specifically he made out more than one woman's voice among them; and he grinned, understanding. Maybe this had been a hotel once, but no longer. Here, in all probability, were the only citizens of Jenny Camp not diverted by the excitement outside, though they were speculating aloud over it; otherwise they wouldn't be talking.

Noiselessly he edged down the hallway, listening by different doors. An unoccupied room, if locked, would give him temporary refuge; what happened then decided on the hand dealt him. Without straining his ears, he could be sure which rooms had occupants, but not which ones might be empty; and now, having reached the end of the hallway, he listened at the last door on his left and, hearing nothing, decided to take the chance.

Carefully he tried the latch. Finding it unlocked, he stepped quickly inside and closed the door. In the same instant, as he stood in total darkness, a match was struck across the room.

Poe wheeled, swinging his gun toward the orange blossom of light. As its thin wash filtered through the dark, he saw a girl sitting up in bed. In one hand she held the flaring match, in the other a little pistol.

She said levelly, "What you do here?"

"Looking for a place to hide. I'm a stranger coming through, and I got shot at. By the whole town, looks like."

"Why? What you do?"

"Nothing. Stopped and had a drink was all."

"Mister, here it takes only that." She nodded at a matchbox on the washstand. "There's matches. You better light the lamp. This match, she's going to go out pretty quick and then maybe I shoot you."

"In the dark?"

"Don' make me nervous. Light it."

Poe said dryly, "Yes, ma'am," and got the matches. Not taking his eyes off her, he lighted the wall lamp one-handed. The light grew in the room, and now, staring at his face, she made a little startled sound.

"*Madre de Dios*," she whispered. "It can't be. He has got a brother, but—no, you're no young enough. Then who are you?"

"Poe Lockhart."

"His pa? You?" She slipped from the bed and came

33

across the room, tipping back her head to study his face. Wonderingly she raised a hand slowly till the fingers almost brushed him. "Yes, it must be. You are just alike. His pa . . . but he say you are in prison."

"Got out. Escaped. You know Gil?"

"I am Gil's girl." She stepped back, eyeing him over. "You big *hombre*, all right. He say you are, but he never say you look like him. Even with the whiskers, is so."

Poe gave her a tired, friendly grin. "Reckon in the real order of things, he looks like me. Mind if I sit down?"

"There is only the bed." She walked back to the rawhide-rigged cot and shoved her small pistol under the pillow. "I keep it there. The doorlock, she's broke." She sat on the edge of the bed and patted the blanket beside her. Poe sat carefully down, the bedframe creaking in protest.

"I am call' Smoky."

The name fit. She was wearing only a camisole, and her skin was the color of tan dusk, smoky-bronze with a gloss of lamplight. She was a bit of a thing, so small-boned and slender she looked almost fragile, but in spite of her frail littleness and huge black eyes in a thin, waiflike face, there was that toughness about her that is born of resiliance to every kind of adversity. The slightness of the girlish roundings that disturbed her worn camisole indicated she was ridiculously young for it, but age meant little in the lot of people like Smoky or Poe Lockhart, who had seen the harsh terms of his own life ingrained before he was old enough to remember. This girl was his own kind—somebody who had been through it all and kept her head toughly up. You were strong enough to make your way or you folded—there was no third choice. The only judgment Poe had ever passed in his life was like or dislike, and such judgments came quickly and surely.

"You got another name?"

" 'Lena. 'Lena Velasco." Childlike, she curled her toes against the cold floorboards, then cocked one slim brown leg across her knee and rubbed her foot, considering. "I'm not 'Lena no more, I guess."

"All right, Smoky. Maybe you can tell me where Gil is."

"Sure, he's over in the valley. You don't know about that, huh?" Poe shook his head. "Well, you see the big cliff back

34

of the town, yes? There is pass through it into valley. There are cabins they have built. That is where they all stay, Dundie and his men. Dundie, he make the women stay over here in the town. He say women in camp alla time would make trouble. He say a few is worse than none because the men would fight over 'em. The men got to visit us over here."

"They don't fight about it here?"

"No, they take turns, except with me. I am Gil's girl only. Tonight he did not—*Dios,* they make plenty racket out there. What you do, anyway?"

A clear drift of voices had lifted from the street outside, as the searching men pulled together in an angry cluster. Poe shrugged. "Like I said, I had a drink across the way. Nobody in there that knew me, and they took a notion I was the law. Reckon they'll be swarming up here in a minute."

"So?"

She stood and went quickly to the window. Pulling back the faded curtains, she tugged up the sash. ". . . turn the goddamn hotel inside out," somebody was saying, as she leaned across the sill and called, "Hey, you tough *hombres,* what's all the noise?"

There were a few laughs and a "Hey, Smoky," and somebody said, "Gil up there? Send him out."

"Gil ain' here. Why can you no keep it quiet?"

Dandy Mack's voice then, chill and ugly: "We're looking for a man. He damn' near broke my head."

"Oh, tha's too bad," Smoky said sympathetically. "Too bad almos', I mean." The men roared, and the redhead's voice said, "Listen—Smoky, any stranger been up there in the last few minutes?"

"I don' know, Shuck. They say all cats is same color in the dark." When the laughter had tapered away, she added, "No, if anybody we don' know come up here, we would make ruckus, huh?"

"That's what I been telling you," the first speaker said impatiently, talking to the others. "If he did come in the hotel the back way, he went out the front. We're wastin' time. One of the empty buildings is where he'd hide. Let's . . ."

Smoky slammed down the sash and grinned at Poe; she

35

walked to the wall where a skirt and blouse hung on a peg. As she slipped them on, she said, "I get Gil and bring him here. You wait for us. Dundie—you know Dundie?"

"He knows me."

"I bring him too. When he tell them fools who you are, they listen good. Don' you leave the room till we come or they shoot you dead, *comprendo?*"

CHAPTER SIX

"Moonlight buggy rides indeed. You know I have choir practice tonight at the church."

Tacey Landrum spoke tartly, but she was far from displeased. Tacey was a small girl of nineteen with a slight, almost boyish figure, but her impact on male senses was nothing if not feminine, Wye Lockhart was firmly convinced. The wonder of it was that she was nearer plain than pretty except for her eyes, wide and violet and full of beautiful shadings. She had a spray of freckles across her nose and cheeks, and a mouth that was soft and too wide, and her shining brown hair was netted in a heavy mass at the back of her neck.

"Well," Wye said soberly, "I'm just a young fellow, you know."

"Oh, fudge!"

"How about eight o'clock sharp?"

"That'll be fine," Tacey said sweetly, "if you want to take me to the church. Do you?"

Wye sighed resignedly. "It's beginning to appear as though I do."

He had met Tacey as she was leaving the Leedstock Mercantile, and now they were walking by the riverbank. "You know," Wye remarked, "we could fool people like the devil."

"What do you mean?"

"Why, we have the loitering air of lovers. Nobody would

36

guess at the iron-plated character of your indecision. That is, about becoming Mrs. Lockhart."

"Well," Tacey sighed, "if they knew just how pestiferous that question had gotten to be—oh, I don't mean you, Wye. You've been wonderfully patient. It's me. I can't stop turning it over in my mind—and I can't decide, either."

"It's as easy as one short word," Wye said gently. "Say yes."

Tacey was silent as they strolled on, hands clasped at her back; she swung her feet half-heartedly at the grass. "It's only—Wye, someday you'll be rich and important."

Wye said matter-of-factly, "Yes," and it sounded pompous enough for him to add, "I hope so."

Since his return from law school a few months ago, Wye had been serving as Sheriff Landrum's deputy, a job to which he had brought a zest and zeal that now had him carrying the bulk of Landrum's duties—and everybody knew it. Landrum's latest term of office would end this fall; rather than run again, he intended opening a drygoods store. Wye, as deputy, would be his logical successor, and Landrum had promised him full support in his bid for election. For sixteen years the office had been to Landrum a comfortable rut; for Wye it would be only a political stepping stone, but a vital one.

As the son of Poe Lockhart, an outlaw whose colorful career had made him a legend around Leedstock and, by avenues of yellow journalism, a sensation across the country, he had a built-in handicap that would haunt him all his life. To offset this background, plus the lesser but now-active reputation of a brother gone bad, a period of direct activity in the service of the law wasn't merely useful but an urgent must. For Wye's goals were high—he had placed no ceiling on them. He meant to go exactly as far as he was politically capable of going, and he had a bitter foretaste of the obstacles he would face as one political opponent after another pounced with glad cries on his antecedents.

"With your dad's help," Wye said, "I'll be off to a good start in the fall. The sheriff's office—then who knows what? Now I ask you—is or isn't that a good and sufficient prospect for Mrs. Wye Lockhart?"

"Of course—if that is what *you* want, Wye. What I don't quite understand is why you're so—well, so intense about it.

As Mr. Fancher's grandson, you'll be a rich man one day without half-trying."

"Wrong," Wye said promptly. "As Gramps' new lawyer, I've seen his will. He's leaving both Gil and me only token amounts. The bulk of the inheritance will go to our half-brother—little Benny Yarbrough, Jr. And Gramps' health being what it is, we'll all be middle-aged before we see a cent of his money. Anyhow, I want to make my own way; that's the heart of my goal, Tace."

"Oh?—And exactly what *is* your goal?"

"To be respected. To pull myself up by my own boot-straps. To make the name of Lockhart into something other than a thief's badge."

Wye's voice held a cold distaste. There was a bitter irony in his knowledge that he owed his outlaw father the superb physique, reflexes, and stamina that fitted him for a lawman's work. From his never-robust mother, though, he had taken what he considered better assets for the long run of things—his finely regular features and dark intense eyes, and a stern habit of examining and sifting his own actions and those of others, lest they be found wanting. Wye felt only a cold contempt for his father's slipshod ethics that had drifted Poe into crime, the disgrace he had forced his family to shoulder and his apparent lack of conscience concerning it.

Tacey said softly, "You're very ashamed of your father, aren't you?"

"Don't tell me you object to that?"

"No-o, it's just that—that everything has to be so perfect with you. I'm a mere girl, Wye; I don't know that I can meet such exacting standards."

"You already do," Wye smiled. "There's not even a question of it."

She shook her head, a trifle impatiently. "But is this what you really feel? I mean, I see so much of what you want, of the things you stand for, as—well, a reaction against your father's reputation."

"I've never denied it," Wye said with a touch of heat. "Is that wrong? To try to replace something infamous with something clean and fine? And I do happen to like the work I've trained myself for. Good Lord, Tace, a man isn't going to plan his whole future just to spite his father's black name.

38

I mean to go far, and I want you at my side—it's as simple as that."

"It's not simple at all," Tacey said sharply. She raised a hand, shading her eyes. "Isn't that Benjy?"

A gig drawn by a brisk-trotting team was coming down the rough freight road that followed the riverbottom to Leedstock. Seeing them, the driver pulled over to the bank. He was a young colored man whose high-yellow face was sweating and impassive; the servant's livery he wore looked ridiculous against a background of backwoods town and dusty flats.

"Mr. Wye, your grandfather sent me to find you. The man from Parkinson's arrived on the three o'clock train."

"The detective? Would that be McKelvey himself, by chance?"

"Yes, sir. Sheriff Landrum brought him to the office, and they're closeted with Mr. Fancher and Mr. Yarbrough."

"Tacey—"

"I know," Tacey said tolerantly. "Anyway, I have to get home and prepare Dad's—look, why don't you have supper with us? The usual time, and you can take me to church afterward."

"To church. Yes, ma'am. Thanks; I'll be there . . . all right, Benjy. Home or his office?"

"The office, sir."

Wye stepped into the gig; he lifted a hand to Tacey's goodbye wave as Benjy swung the vehicle around and headed away from Leedstock on the river road. They went nearly a mile, then turned up a smooth, graveled drive to the Fancher Milling and Mining Company plant. By far the most impressive structure in all this backwoods country, it was a huge single building in the form of a Greek cross on a lonely flat below a timbered mountain flank. A boom of machinery echoed from the main section of the plant as Benjy halted the gig by the entrance to the north wing. This contained the company's sumptuous offices, a monument of lavish ostentation that clashed with the background of heavy industry, raw ore, and sweating labor.

As Benjy clucked the gig team away to the stable, Wye dismounted and went to the entrance where a uniformed watchman gave him a crisp salute of recognition and held open the door. Wye went down a deep-carpeted corridor

39

past rows of gilt-inscribed doors, entered a waiting room and was told by the male secretary to enter the inner office.

This was a tall-ceilinged room, richly paneled, with leaded windows. There was an ornate desk with a crystal lamp and several high-backed chairs. Barrett Fancher stood by a window, hands clasped at his back, looking spectral and frail in a square of harsh sunlight. But his eyes, large and gray and luminous, held a shrewd, youthful dynamism that dominated his narrow, big-browed face and conquered whatever lines age and avarice had placed there.

"Well, Wyatt." He gave that familiar, ascerbic nod. "I'm surprised Benjamin located you so quickly."

Sheriff Clete Landrum was sitting in a chair by the desk, savoring one of Barrett Fancher's excellent cigars. He was a paunchy, middle-aged man with a slack, amiable face, more closely resembling the storekeeper he wanted to be than the undashing lawman he had long been. For that matter, he looked very little like Tacey Landrum's father, though he was. "Wye is got a young man's fancies, Fanch," he said with a mild chuckle. "That does raise hob with his availability."

Wye's stepfather, Ben Yarbrough, gave Wye a grave, sympathetic wink. Yarbrough was leaning against the desk, his arms folded. A man of less than medium height, he had a massive girth that middle age had thickened. Yet he wasn't squat or clumsy; he moved with a muscular grace, and in dress and grooming he was a match for Barrett Fancher who, as Wye knew, had been his example long before Ben's marriage to Wye's mother or Barrett Fancher's gift to Ben of a bank presidency.

Landrum nodded toward the tall man sitting in a gloomy corner of the room, a black Stetson on the floor by his chair. "Bart, this here is Wye Lockhart, my deputy. Barton McKelvey, son."

McKelvey stood and moved forward with none of the slow-jointed stiffness of a man in his late sixties. He was tall, even taller than Wye had visualized him, an erect, gaunt and big-boned man whose years showed in the lined hardness of his bony face and a smooth cap of silvery hair. He wore neat, dead-black clothes that gave him an austere, almost forbidding look. A white mustache followed the humorless droop of his mouth; his eyes were blue, and Wye had heard

40

them described both as icy and steely. Either word applied.

Even if he hadn't known that McKelvey was the officer who had brought in his father six years ago, Wye would have looked forward to this meeting with an eager curiosity. "The Iron Marshal" they had once called him (a title that quickly became "Old Boiler Britches"), and he was building a new reputation as one of Brady Parkinson's top men at an age when most men were content with pipe, slippers, and a surfeit of memories. Parkinson himself headed the Eastern operation of his big, nationwide detective agency from his offices in New York, but he'd shrewdly entrusted charge of all his services in the Southwest to Barton McKelvey.

McKelvey's greeting was a civil nod; his grip was hard and brief and dry. He showed no reaction to Wye's name, and Wye guessed they had prepared him.

Fancher stubbed out his cigar and strode impatiently to the wall behind his desk, saying briskly, "All right, we're all here. Let's get to it, McKelvey."

CHAPTER SEVEN

The old detective moved over to join Barrett Fancher by the huge map that occupied much of the lower wall. It was a platted chart of Leedstock County drawn up from government survey records, with the location of each active mine designated; the Fancher mines were squared in red ink, the handful of their competitors in blue. The chart was scattered with blocks of neatly printed information about each mine and many pertinent matters.

Fancher jabbed a thumb at a mountain area. "This is Jenny Camp. A deserted mining town where Dundie and his pack are supposed to be."

"They are," McKelvey said. "My business is to know, not guess about these things. The Parkinson office in the territory has kept itself informed on Dundie's whereabouts since he crossed back into U. S. territory two months ago. About the time your bullion shipments started getting hit, is that correct?"

41

"Yes," Fancher said in a clipped voice. "You know why I've hired you." His fingers spread on the map raked into a small fist, and he rapped his knuckles on the crackling paper. "I want that nest of thieves cleaned out, but we need proof they're the ones. Find it, McKelvey. I want Dundie behind bars and every one of his pack killed or driven out of the country. I don't care how you get your proof or what it costs—find it."

McKelvey said, "All right," in a dry, unruffled voice. He ran a finger along the map. "You send all your bullion out by rail to Repville. Here's the spur line connecting Repville and Leedstock"—the finger paused—"and the trains are always hit somewhere in the same ten-mile stretch, all mountain country, nothing but a railroad and telegraph line running through, and a horse trail or two."

"Exactly. A stretch of wild, rugged, near-inaccessible country that has to be crossed if Leedstock gold is to be shipped out." Fancher clicked his teeth together. "Let's not rehash what we're both aware of, McKelvey. What can I give you that you need and don't have?"

"A good deal, let's hope. I want to know the date that each holdup occurred, the exact place and the time of day, how much each shipment seized was worth, the number of robbers and how they organized each job, the steps you've taken to thwart them—also names and addresses of witnesses and all other pertinent information."

Fancher opened a drawer of his desk and took out a folder. "I've kept a personal record since the first holdups. Most of what you'll require is in here. I can tell you the rest—that is, concerning our efforts to run the thieves down."

"No luck in picking up their trail, I suppose?"

"None." Facher snapped off a cigar tip between his teeth. "They wear masks and bulky slickers and identical black hats. They split up coming and going and cover every kind of ground—use every conceivable tactic to throw off a tracker. Eventually, of course, all trails converge on Jenny Camp, but not one has been traced there yet."

"And if it were, a single trail wouldn't prove anything," McKelvey muttered, leafing through the contents of the folder. "Ever try setting up a false target?"

"An obvious ruse, sir, and one we've employed

repeatedly, with no success. I've had rumors put out to the effect that a large shipment of gold concentrate, so many thousands of dollars worth, will be shipped out on such-and-such a day. Naturally, the express box is loaded with rocks, and the bona-fide shipment goes out on a later train with absolutely no fanfare. We've tried the trick on three separate occasions and failed each time. The robbers never touched the decoy shipments, just as they've never gone to the trouble of staging a raid for a small amount of bullion. Their strikes are elaborate and well-planned, and always for the large shipments."

"You're aware," McKelvey said in his dry, quiet way, "that somebody has to be leaking information to the robbers. An inside man."

"Damn it, of course I'm aware! But who?" Fancher flung his cigar, unlighted, at a spitoon. "Only four men knew about the decoy shipments. The four of us here—myself, Clete, and Wye as the county law officers, and Ben as president of the Leedstock Bank—my bank—where the bullion is stored after milling and prior to shipping out."

"I assume you have the gold conveyed under guard from your mill to the bank, from the bank to the train."

"Certainly, and the same armed messengers ride escort on the train clear to Repville. But these men were never informed in advance about our plans; they report for duty as they're ordered."

McKelvey's frosty glance rested on the bland, friendly face of the sheriff, on Ben Yarbrough's broad, bearded one, and lastly on Wye's. "Of course you trust the three besides yourself who did have that advance knowledge."

"Implicitly." Fancher's reply was immediate and unhesitating, and his own inclusion in this circle of unquestioned trust set a small pride glowing in Wye. Winning Barrett Fancher's full confidence and a mild measure of his affection had meant overcoming the stigma of suspicion that went with having Poe Lockhart's blood in one's veins. A measure of his triumph was the trust the acid-natured old man now reposed in him.

But McKelvey's chill blue gaze had turned squarely on him, Wye realized uncomfortably. "I mean no offense, Mr. Lockhart, but it's best, when men are to work together, that all cards be laid face-up. You have a brother, two years

43

younger, Gilbert by name, who I understand is up in Jenny Camp with Dundie."

Wye felt his face burn slightly. "Common knowledge, sir."

"Until a month ago," Ben Yarbrough put in quietly, "Gil was working on my ranch. He left after a little difficulty, leaving no word. Then we heard he'd been seen in Jenny Camp. We know nothing more about his recent activities. Certainly Wye has no connection with them and no control over them."

"Nobody could ever control Gilbert's activities," Fancher said cracklingly. "Damned scamp was bound to come to no good—like father, like son." He paused, inspecting the tip of a fresh cigar, and after a moment said with a rare contrition, "Wyatt—I'm sorry, boy. Of course I wasn't implying reference to yourself."

Wye said nothing, feeling the familiar sting of resentment, though he knew the words had been thoughtless, nothing more. The intensity of the feeling made him ashamed and uneasy, and he thought, *That fine madness is the Lockhart in you, my boy—throttle it. Or one day it'll wreck all your plans.*

"Since," McKelvey went on in a tone dry as old leaves, "considering the possibilities close to home seems to get us nowhere, it appears I'll have to focus attention on Dundie himself. I intend to, starting now. You'll forgive me if I don't confide my plans and methods even to you gentlemen. I'm making no accusations, but it's clear that somebody, wittingly or unwittingly, has broken your little circle of confidence."

Fancher nodded briskly. "Makes sense. Do what you have to. I don't care what the cost may be." He finally got to lighting his cigar; he bleakly considered the smoke as it curled up. "Meantime, what sort of protection can you give my outgoing gold shipments?"

"I can load the train with Parkinsons, a small army of our detectives. Enough to fight off any number of outlaws that might try to take it. Oh, I can assure you of getting the gold through." McKelvey's wry pause. "But it's a stopgap solution, you understand—one that a man of your means can doubtless afford, but one whose expense has to be weighed against the value of the article under protection. In

44

addition to our regular fee, we'll bill you for expenses. You'll have to consider your costs in terms of maintaining a regiment of soldiers in the field. How often do you ship out?"

"It depends on varying factors. Oh, once every week to two weeks. Less often, since all this difficulty."

"And in the days between, my men will be idle at your expense. They'll be on active duty only a fraction of the time you're paying us a small fortune for maintaining them here."

"That's not important. I have committments that must be met. Also if the bullion's not sent out, it'll have to be kept in the bank vault until shipping time. I hardly need tell you that the longer it accumulates in one place, the more tempting a target it becomes for anybody with larceny in his heart, not just Dundie. That danger has to be kept to a tolerable level. Fetch your men here, McKelvey, and don't lose a day doing so."

McKelvey inclined his white head "Sheriff, I hope that your office and mine can cooperate to mutual advantage." His unstated meaning was plain; he meant to handle the situation his own way and could do nicely without interference.

Landrum waved a soft, lax hand. "Oh, take as free a hand as you like. No problem there." The sheriff intended to finish out the remainder of his term with as little personal strain as possible.

While Landrum lingered behind to discuss a loan for his new business, Fancher seeming agreeable, Wye and McKelvey and Ben Yarbrough left the building together. Yarbrough climbed to the seat of a spanking new rig tied at a rail. "Pleasant to have met you, sir," he told McKelvey. "Can I offer you a ride to the hotel?"

"Thanks, no. I'm stiffed up from riding the train and would prefer to stretch my legs. Care to walk along, Mr. Lockhart?"

Wye and the old detective walked in silence for a half-minute before Wye ventured, "I've wanted for years to meet you, sir. I've admired you since I was a small boy."

McKelvey swung a harsh and quizzical stare against his face. "Oh? Perhaps I was wrong. I'd guessed you knew I was the man who brought in your father six years back."

"Of course I knew." Wye felt suddenly callow and

abashed. "It's just that I admire the law and its workings above anything. I hope to serve in the judicial and legislative side myself—but if I can be a fraction of the man you've been in a lifetime of the active side of law enforcement, I'll be satisfied."

"Thank you," McKelvey said dryly. "Since we're working together, I'd wanted to talk to you privately—in case you felt any resentment toward me because of your father. It would be a quite normal and understandable feeling, Mr. Lockhart. I see there'll be no need." After a pause, he added abruptly, "Understand this about the law, young fellow. It's a rough-hewn tool fashioned by men— fallible men—largely out of old superstitions and blind customs and piecemeal improvisations. Serve it, but don't let it become your god."

Wye's cheeks smarted. "I haven't—"

"Haven't you, Mr. Lockhart? I would hazard a guess why, but a word to the wise should suffice. You're a bright young fellow. Don't let a sorry memory or two cause you to act the fool. There's a danger of that—think about it awhile."

Wye held an angry silence the whole distance to town. From all he'd ever heard of McKelvey, he had believed the man was driven by an all-consuming devotion to the law, and had felt akin to him for this reason. Tacey was a girl and he could laugh at her girlish doubts when she voiced them; yet McKelvey had just stated Tacey's misgivings in a different way.

As they came into Leedstock's central street, Wye saw old Bowie from the telegraph office hurry across the street to the combination sheriff's office and jail; he began pounding on the door. Wye hailed him, and Bowie came over, his old face wry and cross.

"Where's Clete at?"

"Out at Fancher's mill," Wye said. "If that telegram's business, I'll take it to him."

"Business all right," Bowie said, and slapped the yellow paper into Wye's palm and walked away. The telegram was longer than most; Wye read it quickly through and felt a stunned coldness in the pit of his belly. Not trusting his voice, he handed the paper to McKelvey without a word.

It was a half-minute before McKelvey spoke; his tone

46

held a bitter control. "So your pa broke out of Coldrock a whole week ago."

Wye said defensively, "I didn't know!"

"Wasn't inferring you did. The part that concerns me is that Tom Rydell, Coldrock's head tracker, went after your pa and hasn't been seen since. The prison officials gave Rydell this much time before releasing the news. A whole week—you know what that could mean?"

Wy said bitterly, "I suppose that something happened to Rydell."

"It means more than that, boy." McKelvey's eyes were ironlike; so was his grip on Wye's arm. "Tom Rydell was my deputy for years; he was a careful man. If anything happened to him, somebody made it happen. Now I want you to think—do you have any idea at all where your father might have gone or where he is now. Wait." McKelvey snapped his fingers. "Did he know about your brother joining Dundie?"

"He could have, I suppose. Ben Yarbrough kept him regularly posted on things—"

McKelvey said softly, "That's it," and pivoted on his heel, heading for the livery stable. After a hesitating moment, Wye went after him with an irritable, "Wait."

Not halting, McKelvey said grimly, "I came here on the train; I'll need a horse," and strode on into the stable. He handed the hostler a bill. "That'll take care of a horse and saddle for two days. I'll pick my own."

Wye said, "Look—if it's to be Jenny Camp, I know these parts. I can show you the way."

McKelvey gave a dry, wintry chuckle. "Sonny, they'd eat you alive up there." He walked to the saddle pole and chose a heavy rig; he bridled and saddled a sorrel gelding. "Jenny Camp was in its prime ten years before you saw light of day, and I knew it then."

"I'm supposed to be working with you," Wye said bitterly.

"I don't count this a job so much as a personal thing," McKelvey said across his shoulder as he adjusted the latigo. "Tom is a good friend. Is or was. I propose to learn which. Besides I need to find out all I can about Dundie's outfit, and this is a chance to size it up."

"But the risk—alone!"

47

"No risk unless I push it. Dundie's not fool enough to let a Parkinson man get killed in his town. Mr. Brady P. would leave no stone unturned to get the man responsible—and Dundie knows it. One detective won't be too bothersome, but two of us riding in might cut things loose. Besides—" McKelvey paused dryly— "self-righteous folks are too damned proddy. They can't help asking for trouble."

Wye flushed. "Thanks for your confidence. The fact remains that it's my job—"

"Your job," McKelvey said flatly, "is to tell the sheriff where I've gone and why. Do it."

He swung to the saddle and reined the horse down the runway and into the street. Wye saw him dismount by the hotel and go inside. In a few minutes, he emerged carrying saddlebags and a blanket roll which he secured to his saddle. Mounting then, he took the north road out of town.

CHAPTER EIGHT

Dundie leaned across the table, refilling Poe's glass from a bottle of excellent Scotch. The two of them were sitting in a back corner of Alabam's place where they were slightly isolated from the boisterous swell of talk, laughter, noise that filled the room. It was early afternoon, but Dundie's boys and their few women kept no regular hours.

"Ye know," Dundie remarked, "the resemblance between you and Gil is no less than remarkable, more so now you've removed the beard."

Poe had been surprised himself, after bathing and shaving and dressing in the well-worn Levi's and shirt Gil had given him, to find the clothes only a couple sizes too small. A few more pounds and Gil would be his image. Even the runover half-boots his son had provided fit his outsize feet perfectly.

"A tough break, your killing a lawman." Dundie gazed speculatively into his drink. "Even if it was an accident. . . ."

48

Poe said mildly, "If it's got you worried, I can ride on, Clem."

Dundie leaned back, coughing delicately against the back of his wrist. He was a youngish-seeming man, tall but slightly built, almost boyish except for a ravaged elegance in his manner. His light bland eyes in a bony, freckled, sunburned face were flickering with temper, for Poe's suggestion had touched his pride. He coughed again, squinting against the furling smoke of a thin cigar in his mouth which was given a droll twist by a crescent-shaped scar at one corner. He wore soiled white flannels and a wide-brimmed panama hat from beneath which his flaming red hair stuck out in awry tufts.

"Why, no, Poe, I wouldn't want that. I admit to an aversion to killing, especially lawmen, an antipathy I picked up from you years ago—but nobody can prove a thing, can they? However I'd like to know exactly how ye knew enough to ride straight here after your escape. Prison grapevine?"

"Ben Yarbrough kept in touch. He mentioned your being back in Jenny Camp. In the same letter he told me about Gil throwing in with you."

"Well, isn't that fine." Dundie let smoke dribble across his teeth. "A thoughtful man, Mr. Yarbrough. Few in his place would be as considerate—I mean with the matter of your wife between you. By the way, I'm curious as to your feeling about the boy coming in with us."

Dundie's offhand manner belied the sharpness of his stare, but Poe had been expecting the question. "How am I supposed to feel, Clem?"

"Well, ye always did think the world of those boys of yours. As I recall, you made a good deal of seeing that they received a proper rearing by your wife."

"They were kids then. They had a right to learn about every side. Just as Gil has a right to choose his, now he's grown."

"That sounds reasonable. Parental, no—but reasonable." Dundie gave a jaded chuckle. "I suppose you know your older boy is deputizing for Clete Landrum."

"Hadn't known before Gil said so. Last mention Ben made of Wye was that he'd just returned from law school."

Dundie nodded lazily. "Took you sort of by surprise, eh?

49

Ye ken the complications—you and the lad could wind up shooting at each other. Or he and Gil could. Regular brother's war, eh?"

Poe followed Dundie's idle glance across the room to where Gil sat at a table playing stud, scowling in concentration at his fistful of cards. His face was already heavy and hard-ridged with young maturity. Roll back the scene some twenty-odd years to any roadhouse on the Chisholm, any hellhole in the heyday of Abilene and Ellsworth, and this could be the young Poe Lockhart; even the stamp of his fellow players matched the brand of companion Poe had always managed to find.

The members of Dundie's gang ran to a familiar pattern, a single name or nickname serving to identify each. None of it was new to Poe except the gray distaste that filled his mouth. He had lied about his feelings to Dundie, but he could not for an instant pretend to himself.

Smoky stood behind Gil's chair, one hand cocked on her hip, the other toying with a fantail of shaggy hair behind her ear. She met Poe's gaze over his head and a defiance touched her small face, as if, in spite of their friendliness last night, she thought he might be disapproving of her now. She laid her cheek against Gil's hair and glared impudently. *Do I look that much like a doting daddy?* Poe wondered with a wry amusement. Too independent to give a damn about social labels, he liked tough little Smoky; he sensed that she felt similarly toward Gil: whatever he might or might not be, he was her man. Poe grinned at her and lifted his glass in mild assurance; Smoky grinned too.

Last night, after she had returned with Dundie and Gil, and Dundie had damped down the gang's anger and introduced Poe all around, Poe and his son had sat in Gil's tarpaper shack and talked deep into the morning hours, passing a bottle back and forth. Though bothered by Gil's obvious idolizing of his outlaw past, Poe had also found a man-to-man camaraderie more pleasurable than anything he could remember. There was a wry irony in the knowledge that though he was here to wean Gil away from his present life, he could enjoy with this son a meaty man's talk, seasoned by rough-and-tumble fun that he could never have found with Wye, who was jacketed in his repectability.

Gil had clarified Wye's attitudes—if any clarification had

50

been needed. Wye had repudiated everything having to do with his father's memory, fashioning his own life and prospects in opposition to it. Gil seemed less indignant than puzzled by the whole situation, for in spite of their differences, the two brothers had always gotten along. "His soul-saving goddamn ways was like to make me puke sometimes," Gil had admitted, "but all the same he stuck by me, Pa. I know for sure some of the bullshit I pulled embarrassed hell out of him, but he was always there to step for me, no matter what."

Wye had his mother's stern sense of duty, Poe reckoned, and was careful to avoid the least hint of his own purpose for coming here. Making noises like a sky pilot would never win Gil over; he needed to get to know his son first, then decide what might be done.

"Ye know," Dundie was saying, "I wasn't sure at first, but you've changed."

Poe was staring absently at his glass; he snapped back to focus, then lifted his eyes to meet Dundie's dry, curious look. "How's that?"

"Why, I hardly know how, Poe—it's just there, ye ken. You're no less tough and you'll still go it your own way if it kills ye, of that I'm sure. You're a good deal quieter than you were, but prison does that to a man, I'm told. No, it's a deeper thing, as if some of the wildness has gone out of you."

Poe dropped his gaze to his scarred knuckles, saying mildly, "Maybe a man gets tamed in there, Clem. Among other things, he's got time to think—for instance about who passed the word to the law that got him buried in a two-by-four cell."

Poe's feeler was an idle one, but he was not discounting a possibility of Dundie being the man who had betrayed him. Of the gang, he had told Dundie and a couple of others close to him that he was going to Yarbrough's that night; it wasn't the sort of thing he would spread wholesale beyond those few he had trusted absolutely. Only now, with the deep-dyed cynicism ingrained by six years of prison living would he make the harsh concession that nobody deserved a man's complete trust.

Dundie interpreted the remark as it was intended; his eyes narrowed. "Well, Poe, if your thinking leans that way,

51

you had better say it out straight. Are ye thinking it?"

"Not one way or the other yet," Poe said gently. "If I ever do think it, Clem, you won't need to ask."

"Fair enough." Dundie blew smoke upward; his pride could not let Poe's last comment pass unheeded, so he added, "Good to have ye back, lad. Just so you remember who's the dog now leads the pack. Do ye conceive me?"

Poe shrugged. "All right with me, Clem. You know I never liked it."

"That's true; ye never did." Dundie's point was made; he was genial again. "You were always a lone wolf by instinct. The boys looked to you for leadership, but you never felt comfortable with it." He flicked ash off his cigar; his eyes were remote. "Know where I've spent the last six years?"

"Mexico was all I heard."

"True enough. As soon as word of your capture reached us, the gang broke up and cleared out. A few of us hung together for a time; we passed into Sonora and frequented roadhouses no better than rattraps, reveling amid the putas and the pulque, becoming marked by what good folk describe as 'low dissipations.' To make money, I led other tough ones in short, swift raids across the border on American ranches; we drove back small bunches of cattle and sold them to an incurious *ranchero* near Hermosillo. The experience whetted my own taste for leadership, and Mexico furnished a likely setting to outfit an old ambition of mine."

Dundie rocked back in his chair, steepling his fingers. "When I was a lad in Ayr County, living in a hut by the coal pits, I'd steal up to the laird's manor on the hill and fill my eyes with its grandeur by the hour. Down in Mexico, I found an old daydream reawakened by thousands of acres of cheap empty land, room for a man to build and grow. To cut the story short, I became a citizen of Mexico and made the dream concrete; I gained a respectable wife and a bairn too, and a raggedy lot of peons who call me Don Clement. But I fell on hard times—drought—and it takes money to maintain a feudal empire, even in Mexico. Returning to the old haunts to raid Barrett Fancher's bullion shipments— plums ye'd never permit us to touch in the old days—was the answer. I had no difficulty in collecting about me a gang of Anglos for the enterprise—other Americans who had come to Sonora for more or less my own original reasons, all fed up to their necks with greaser grub, greaser hooch, and greaser women—God damn Mexico. Ungrateful *chingados*."

As he spoke, Dundie sent a glance of cold disgust around the room; clearly he felt only affection for the land where he had realized a dream. He was a strange man, proud and wry, as candid as he was dishonest, completely aware of his own contradictions; the sides of his nature were everlastingly at war, and Poe could understand how that was.

Dandy Mack McMurdo was leaning against the bar, sipping whiskey while he eyed Poe with an unconcealed malice. Dundie said, "McMurdo's head'll be sore for a long while. No need to tell you to watch your back when he's about." He did not sound very concerned; his shrewd eyes were appraising Poe now. "You know, I learned a good deal from you, laddie, but ye made your mistakes. Hitting too often and too far from home was one of them; I keep operations on a narrower scale. Officialdom isn't happy about me, but not too mad either; they can't prove anything and they'll not try too hard to do so unless a public clamor forces their hand."

Dundie quit talking; his glance found the doorway where a flint-faced man in a ragged jumper had just entered, pausing to accustom his eyes to the smoke-filled gloom of the room after coming out of bright sunlight. "That's Pima Jack," Dundie said. "By day I keep a couple of men posted on the heights well above the camp where they can command every trail. A minor precaution. Jack has the best pair of eyes among us."

Dundie raised a hand to catch the half-breed's attention, but Pima Jack had already spotted him and was threading through the room's occupants to reach their table. He was a small man, scarred and calloused and sun-blackened; he said, "Man comin' on the trail. From Leedstock way."

"Oh?" Dundie's lifting hand halted the cigar short of his lips. "Get a sight of his face?"

"I see. It's old McKelvey. He comin' alone."

"Well. Well." Dundie was not an easy man to surprise, but he looked mildly incredulous. "A visit from old Boiler Britches. I wonder if . . . no. If he had anything on us, he'd

53

come in with an army at his heels." His glance pounced swiftly on Poe. "Would he be looking for you?"

"It's likely." Poe started to push to his feet. "I better get out of sight, Clem."

"No. Stay where ye are." A cold smile touched Dundie's narrow face. "Not a United States marshal any more, is he—McKelvey? Very well; there's one authority up here—mine. And no damned gumshoe of Brady Parkinson's is going to walk in and read the rules for my town."

Pima Jack edged over to the bar, his dark stoic's face alert; he signaled Alabam to pour him a drink. The noise of the room had dimmed, and now it trickeled into near-silence as everybody watched Dundie, waiting his word.

"Ignore him," Dundie said.

The talk picked up, underkeyed, and with no punctuations of laughter. When the batwing doors parted and the tall, gaunt man in black stepped through them, there was a careful disregard of him. McKelvey paused on the threshold for the fleeting moments it took him to condition his eyes and spot Poe at the back table. He moved down the room toward them. In six years he had gotten leaner and grayer; Poe could discern no other change in him.

Dundie made a spare yet studied gesture of removing the cigar from his mouth. "Want to see me, detective?"

"In my good time," McKelvey murmured. "Stand up, Lockhart."

He pulled his gun as he spoke, and cocked and leveled it at Poe, all in a smooth motion. Again the room quieted down, this time abruptly.

McKelvey spoke gently into the stillness; "You're wearing Tom's gun. I'd know it in a thousand. And you'd never have taken it unless it was off his dead body."

CHAPTER NINE

Poe was careful not to move; he kept both hands flat on the table, but he did not obey McKelvey's order. He had considered abandoning Rydell's pistol, but no other handgun had been available, and going unarmed in Jenny Camp had seemed riskier than wearing the gun with its distinctively checkered grips. He shuttled a glance at Dundie, who only looked bored.

"Do you have anything like a body, McKelvey? Witnesses, perhaps?"

"The gun's enough to arrest him on suspicion of murder."

"Now," Dundie said ominously, "who are you to be arresting anybody, gumshoe? Don't. I know who Brady Parkinson is. But just don't stretch it, McKelvey."

"I won't tell you again," McKelvey said with a stiff undernote of danger, "to stand up, Lockhart. Then shuck that gun."

A shot crashed out on the heels of his words. McKelvey's pistol was smashed from his hand as if an unseen club had been swung; it boomed against the log wall and clattered to the floor.

Halfway across the room Gil Lockhart straddled a chair, one arm laid across its back and his other arm braced straight across it, holding a pistol at arm's length. His aim had been careful; now he slowly lowered the gun, his eyes reckless and pleased. "The Lockharts send regards to Mr. Brady Parkinson."

McKelvey was bent over hugging his hurt hand, his face set and bloodless. Now he gradually straightened, pulled upright by his iron will; his gray and wintry stare was tight on Gil. He said shallowly, "You'll find that was a mistake, boy."

"Not half as bad as the one you near made if you had gone and pulled that trigger, mister—"

"You'd better tell him to finish it, Dundie," McKelvey cut in savagely. "By God, you'd better."

"Hardly." Dundie eyed the tip of his cigar almost with distaste. "Letting one of Brady Parkinson's operatives come to harm in my town could be suicidal, as we're both fully aware, McKelvey. Parkinson makes it his brag that nobody takes out a Parkinson man and gets away with it— and he makes his word good, as everybody knows."

Poe was sensitive to a low rise of temper sweeping the crowd. Some of the men were talking in underpitched voices. No officer in the territory had been more feared and hated

55

during his career than McKelvey. There were those present who could trace the time they had served in prison directly to this man's own efforts. Even hearing his name spoken stirred their hackles; with the man himself disarmed and helpless before them, they were going to be hard to control.

It was Dandy Mack McMurdo who crowded the moment, pushing away from the bar with a damp smile. "Let's don't be hasty, Clem. Likely nobody knows he came here; he always was a lone wolf."

McKelvey's glance swiveled on him. "That's sense, boy. You go ahead. Kill me. Then hunt up Wye Lockhart and kill him, because he knows I'm here. Then you'll have to kill Clete Landrum because Lockhart would have told him. Then maybe half the town of Leedstock because you can't be sure who else'll know by now, can you?"

Dandy Mack glazed his eyes, grinning. "Bluff."

"Damn you, McMurdo!" Dundie crashed his fist on the table. "Killing him would draw on our heads the very trouble I've fought to avoid. I say no!"

The room grew still. The situation was swaying on a hair's-breadth because nobody had overtly sided with Dundie. Poe pushed back his chair and came to his feet, swinging away from the table to face McMurdo.

Dandy Mack's eyes were wicked and warning. "It's your neck he's after, Lockhart. Are you backing up Clem?"

Poe nodded.

"You crossed me last night too, Brother Lockhart," Dandy Mack said. "I wouldn't again."

"You opened the ball last night," Poe told him. "You can open this one too."

Now Gil wordlessly stood and came over to range himself beside Poe. A thin commotion rustled through the room as men took up talk and movement again. Somebody said, "I heard a hell of a good story." The moment was ended, and Dandy Mack turned in a fury back to the bar. Poe felt the sharp puzzlement of McKelvey's stare on him.

Dundie did not relax; he pointed his finger like a gun barrel at the detective. "McKelvey, you got lucky. Don't think on this account you can crowd a man too far. By God, if you come again into my town—my town, ye ken?—and try to play the little lone god, you can shake Brady Parkinson or the devil himself at me, and it won't save ye."

"I'll come," McKelvey said tonelessly. "When I do, it'll be on a different errand. And when I leave, you'll be leaving too, dead or alive."

Dundie smiled. His pride had blazed and was satisfied, and had sheathed itself. "Poe, you'd better escort our visitor safely away from Jenny Camp. There seem to be a few people around wanting to have a shot at him. That may come in time—not yet. Oh, Gil, would ye hand the gumshoe his property? I wouldn't like him to have a real excuse for coming back, such as a broken gun he'd left behind."

Grinning, Gil scooped up the wrecked pistol and passed it to McKelvey who took it wordlessly and rammed it in his belt. Poe nodded at McKelvey then, and the detective wheeled and strode out ahead of him. Leaving McKelvey at the hitchrail, Poe walked down to the end of town and the pasture and ramshackle corral that held the gang's horses. He started to rope out the bay that had been Rydell's before he remembered; he roped and saddled a blazeface sorrel instead. He would have to ask Dundie for a new horse and take the bay into the hills and turn him loose.

Stepping into the saddle, Poe rode back to Alabam's, thinking grimly, *If the old bastard asks me is this Rydell's horse too, I'll make him stuff it, by God.* McKelvey, sitting his horse and waiting, made no comment at all; he ranged his mount alongside Poe's, and they rode out of Jenny Camp together.

McKelvey said presently, "Suppose I ought to thank you."

Poe shrugged. "Clem was right was all. Why beg for trouble?"

"That won't wash in your case," McKelvey observed. "You've already found all the trouble your case can stand, boy. I think you did for Tom Rydell, and I'll follow you to hell if I have to. Don't you know that?"

Poe reined in and quartered the sorrel roughly around, grabbing McKelvey's bridle. "Maybe we should settle this right now," he said thinly. "Sooner or later it'll have to be that way."

"That's right," McKelvey agreed. "Why not do the job while I'm in no case to argue? I can't use a sore hand even to hold a broken gun. That's assuming you were disposed to give me an even break."

Poe settled back slowly in his saddle; his hand dropped from the rein and there was a coldness of defeat in his belly. All he could do now was tell McKelvey the whole truth of what had happened and trust to his shrewdness for assessing a man's word and his fair judgment. It made a thin enough hope.

"I want to talk," he said quietly. "I'll tell how it happened. But let's ride on." He gave a faint nod at the stony ridges that lifted to either side. "There's at least one man posted up there watching us. Keep riding."

McKelvey's eyes were pale and cold in his hatbrim shadow; not moving his head, he swept the heights with his glance. Poe could see him filing away this piece of information against any future use. The detective nudged his horse forward; they rode apace on the trail.

"I'm listening. So Rydell is dead?"

Poe told it all, quietly and dispassionately: Rydell's capture of him and the trick he'd turned that had resulted in the tracker's death. "I'll tell you the place if you want."

"No need." McKelvey's tone was quiet and positive. "I know how you always avoided gunplay in the old days. I'm inclined to believe this happened as you said. Rydell was a good man, but he was a manhunter and he had his eyes open—a manhunter goes into it knowing the game can break against him any time. Don't ask me why, but the danger's part of the candle that draws him." McKelvey sounded almost offhand; he added, "I want to know just one thing. If it hadn't been an accident, if you'd had the open choice of taking a man's life in order to make good an escape, would you?"

Poe shook his head. "I don't know. I wondered about it plenty, but I can't tell you what I can't answer for myself. I sure as hell wish it hadn't happened, but it did and it's done."

"All right. Lockhart, before this, I've seen men you could almost draw a clean line down the middle of their character, right on one side, wrong on the other—but you're the fence-straddler of the lot. Let me tell you now—society has no use for straddlers; society needs to be sure of a man. You talk like a man who's changed. Have you changed or not?"

Poe only shrugged, and McKelvey said a trifle wearily, "All right, you say you broke prison and came here to find

58

your boy and try to talk him off the trail he's on. That sounds reasonable, but let's carry it a step farther—to Poe Lockhart. If it hadn't been for Gil, would you have gone back to the old life?"

"No, but that don't signify a man's changed any. It's just—" Poe paused, frowning over what he wanted to say —"what did it get me before? Turned my wife and my oldest boy against me—then these six years in prison. I had my reasons for taking up outlawing, but maybe if I'd held on a little longer with the ranch, things would've turned for the better. Be different if I had it to do over—but knowing what I do now, that's plain damned good sense, no more."

McKelvey's chuckle was very dry. "Son—all that stands between about ninety percent of the race and utter perfidy is that good sense you mention. Man who conducts his daily life for the reasons he hears given in church every Sunday is about as common as hen's teeth."

"Why," Poe said dryly, "I suspicion you might be a hen's tooth. That damnfool play back there of pulling a gun on me with Dundie's bunch all around you—damned if that wasn't a hen's tooth man's doing. I'd swear you believe in something, McKelvey."

"All I did," McKelvey said metallically, "was something no lawman worth his salt ever should: lost control of myself because I saw you wearing Tom's gun. About your boy, now—persuaded him any?"

"I ain't tried. It'll take time."

"Time you won't be allowed," McKelvey declared harshly. "Lockhart, I'm going to break this gang into pieces; if your boy gets caught with the rest, he'll pull as stiff a sentence as any of them. At that he might be lucky—if he keeps on with them awhile, he could catch a bullet. Or collect a string of offenses that'll get him a noose or life imprisonment. All kinds of things could happen to him, Lockhart, and none of them good."

By now they had ascended a wooded hillflank and were deep in the concealing timber. Poe halted and so did McKelvey, meeting his stare. Poe said flatly, "If something's on your mind, get it out."

McKelvey leaned forward in his stirrups. "I want to make a trade with you. Here's the offer: minimum prison sentences for both you and your son. You'll have to stand trial for killing Rydell—no compromises there. But the help you can give us, along with my influence thrown behind you, can make a lot of difference—even to a governor's pardon."

Poe eyed him impassively. "What's your slice of it, McKelvey?"

The detective countered his question with another: "I want to be sure of one thing. There's no doubt in your mind—your boy's welfare comes first and last with you?"

"I told you."

McKelvey began to talk swiftly now, sketching out what he had in mind. In order to take Dundie and his gang, he had to catch them with the goods. So far the fish had proven too slippery to net because somebody was clearly leaking to Dundie information known by only four men: Ben Yarbrough, Clete Landrum, Wye Lockhart, and Barrett Fancher himself. One of them, or somebody close to them, had to be the guilty party.

McKelvey's idea was to infiltrate Dundie's gang with an inside man of his own, one who could feed out the knowledge that would enable him to pinpoint the gang's guilt and trap them cold. He had planned to use one of his own field operatives for the job.

The trouble was that any man undertaking a deception of this nature found it as much as his life was worth to carry it off convincingly. First he needed the background and training for the role, and it was helpful if he had a genuine shady spot or two in his own past. Even if he gained the gang's confidence enough to be admitted to the inner councils, he would be under surveillance and suspicion for a long time; he would tiptoe on eggs in the knowledge that his first misstep would be his last. Moreover, establishing such a setup would take weeks and months, and the results were always uncertain.

"You've guessed the rest by now," McKelvey said quietly. "That's what I'm trading for—all you can learn that would enable us to break up Dundie's operation and put him and his bunch behind bars. And I can't wait on your answer, Lockhart; I'm moving hard and fast, and it has to be now."

A full minute went by as Poe sat his saddle unspeaking, his head bent. McKelvey's blunt offer had forced him to an awareness of something he had shunned meeting face-on

60

until now: that any possibility of his convincing Gil to break with the gang was almost nil.

At last McKelvey said with transparent disgust, "Why all the hesitation? Code of the outlaw? Christ, you of the brotherhood are like a secret lodge or kids playing at pirate, signing the oath in their blood. What do you owe Dundie or any of them? I had you pegged as too independent for that nonsense."

"That's right," Poe said with an edge. "Enough so nobody tells me my way. Neither do you. Shut your damned mouth and let me think it out."

McKelvey seemed pleased; his granitic face twitched to the faintest of grins, and he was silent and waiting then. Poe was far from as self-assured as his speech suggested; thought of betraying the gang sat badly in his craw, but on the other hand he felt no personal inclination to return to the old life, and he felt no real loyalty to Dundie who he knew had given him sanctuary to puff his own confidence. Overriding all other considerations was Poe's determination to see Gil's outlaw career nipped in the bud, and now he could admit to himself that McKelvey had shown him the only sure way.

He said at last, "All right—we'll try it your way," and eyed the detective narrowly. "You were taking a hell of a long chance, giving away your scheme about putting a man inside Dundie's gang. Suppose I hadn't gone along?"

McKelvey smiled frostily. "Then I'd have thought of something else. As I saw 'em, the odds weren't so long. Your son comes first with you, and I minded how you'd taken my part today when you might have done better to side with the others against Dundie. He has a reason for not wanting me gunned down in his town—you'd have been a sight better off seeing me fixed so I couldn't dog your trail any more. The change is there all right—up to you where it takes you from here."

Barton McKelvey paused, his gaze pale and stark now. "Whole thing rides on you now, Lockhart. You'll need to be damned careful. So will I; this stays between us two, because if that inside man learns what's up, you're as good as dead."

"Want me to try to learn who he is?"

McKelvey stroked his silvery mustache; he shook his

head. "No, too risky. I've a hunch Dundie alone knows his identity. Besides I think our best bet's to crush the body of the snake—the gang itself. Dundie'll be telling his men the plan for their next operation; when he does, you'll get word to me as soon as possible."

"How?"

"Let's see . . . best if you don't ride into Leedstock." McKelvey pointed at a monument of red stone among the rocky heights to the southeast, perhaps five miles in the direction of Leedstock. "Under that tall rock will do. I'll come there twice a week, Wednesday and Saturday afternoons at two o'clock. As soon as you know, you'll meet me." He paused. "Will you have any trouble getting away?"

Poe shook his head. "Everybody comes and goes from Jenny Camp like he pleases. What if I find out too late for waiting? How do I get you word right away?"

"Nothing for it then but to ride into town and hunt me up. I'll stay as close to the hotel as possible, but if you can't locate me, leave some kind of message."

Poe nodded, then lowered his stare to his horse's mane. "McKelvey—how is he? Wyatt?"

McKelvey shrugged. "Why, proud of standing against everything you stood for. Or did you know that?" Poe only nodded, and McKelvey said, "Saturday then—if," and turned his horse down the trail.

CHAPTER TEN

Wye Lockhart tipped his head back to smell the air. The sky was streaky with bad weather; across the valley a gray gauze of rain was falling on the foothills. He dropped his chin and looked at Tacey Landrum beside him, then at the guards from the Fancher mill laboriously wrestling a heavy box out of a wagon pulled up at the railroad siding. Three of them loaded the box into the express car while two more stood by with ready rifles.

Wye did not take his eyes off the loading now until it was

finished and three of the guards were inside the car. The door was clanged shut and locked by the two outside men. Afterward they climbed into the wagon bed and the driver clucked to his team and swung the wagon around, heading back to drop off the two remaining guards where they were both needed: at the Fancher mill and at Leedstock's crackerbox of a bank.

At last Wye looked again at Tacey, surprising a somber worry in her eyes. There had been a constraint between them since that day last week when they'd talked by the river; her frankness had been abrasive to his pride. Now he saw her unguarded concern for him, and felt a pleasure, even a relief.

"Only three guards," she said. "And you and Dad. It won't be enough, Wye, if—"

"*If* the odds are too heavy," Wye said in a positive tone, "we don't intend getting suicidal, Tace. Have the robbers killed anyone yet?"

"Just plain luck they haven't, I should say. There could be a first time—any time. And it would be like you to refuse to give up, even if—"

"Well," came Clete Landrum's hearty voice, "come to see us off, honey?" The sheriff had arrived at a brisk stride, stocky and round-shouldered in his neat black suit. The big Spencer .56 buffalo rifle he carried under one arm looked bulky and incongruous.

Tacey hugged him. "Take care—and take care of your deputy. When will you be back?"

Landrum patted her shoulder. "In two days, about. Be just fine, honey; it'll all go fine as frog's hair, and you ain't to worry, hear?"

He kissed her goodbye, and moved off toward the passenger coach, calling hello to the brakie down by the caboose. There was a gray specter behind Clete's heartiness, but then he was always nervous when an important job was underway, Wye knew. Clete would have been contented to run for sheriff to his dying day if the job had offered nothing more harrowing than jailing a friendly drunk now and then; yet he was a man who always swallowed his fear when the chips were down.

Wye glanced along the line of cars. As usual the train consisted of a locomotive and tender, a couple of flatcars loaded with timbers, the passenger and baggage-express

63

cars, a pair of freight cars which Wye had checked and found empty, and a caboose. Woody Kline, the brakeman-conductor, came walking past from the caboose. "You kids want to spoon fare-thee-well, best get to it. We'll be moving in a minute."

Wye and Tacey moved forward to the passenger coach. Here Wye turned, still feeling a thread of awkward constraint, some of it stemming from an increasing tension over the job ahead. He said, "Well—goodbye," watching her soberly. Tacey made an odd little purr of impatience in her throat. "Oh, Wye! Here—" She reached up and pulled his head down and kissed him. He felt the slight yet impudent curves of Tacey's slim body press warm and alive through their clothing. He tasted the softness of her lips, then a startling hint of moist passion that made his arms tighten.

The engine gave a chugging hiss; the drivers churned ponderously and the cars jerked and slammed on their couplings. Wye broke away and swung aboard, lifting a jaunty hand to Tacey as the wheels rumbled into motion.

Leaving the vestibule, Wye walked the length of the coach which was empty but for himself and the sheriff. He dropped into the seat facing Landrum, who gave him a nod and a determined grin that didn't lessen the worry deepening the slack creases of his face.

Wye laid his Winchester across his knees and studied the drab flats whisking by. He felt moody again, and the gunmetal texture of this day did nothing to abate the feeling. He was sure that Tacey loved him, yet she was unsure of herself and of him too. *One of us will have to change,* he thought grimly. *It'll have to be her—I don't even want to.*

Landrum shifted his rifle from his right to his left hand and tugged a bandanna from his pocket; the car was drafty and not warm, but he mopped his face. He muttered, "Damn that McKelvey. Them detectives of his should of been here by today."

By now this was a familiar complaint of his, but Wye half-absently took the trouble to answer. "Can't put blame on him for that. He wired for the men. The nearest force of Parkinsons available was at St. Louis, and they're being sent. If something held them up, no fault of his."

"Maybe not, but that don't help our case if something

64

happens this trip. After saying we should be on the train today, least he could of done was come along himself."

"Well, he wanted to go check on what's holding up his men. We know from the telegram his agency sent that they were on their way here."

"Pretty thin damn reason for leaving yesterday like he done," Landrum grumbled. "He knew this big shipment was going out today. Your gramps was damn good and mad, and can't say I blame him. He was worried about all that bullion accumulating in the bank—and all McKelvey would say when Fanch asked him should he go ahead and ship today, was, 'Keep everything on schedule.' That detective is too independent by half. Least a man could do is confide his goddamn plans a decent spell ahead."

"Well, you know he's used to playing his hand alone." Wye's voice was patient; he knew that Clete would steady down if and when things started popping. "He told us at the start he wouldn't take chances even on the four of us, you and Ben and me, and even Gramps. He didn't mince words, and we all went along."

Landrum growled, "Even so," and slacked morosely back in his seat, dropping his hat over his eyes, leaving Wye to his own thoughts. After a while Wye's mood blurred somewhat and so did the thoughts; he half-slept as the train rocked and jolted upward, crawling past the foothills into the peaks.

When he finally woke with a start, Wye at once looked out the window. They were high up, all right, rocketing up a narrow sweep of dynamite-cleft roadbed in the flank of a mountain; and off left of them the tortuous contour of Windigo Pass dropped to dizzying depths obscured by a milky mist. They were close to the edge of the wild country where, sometime in the next two hours, they would learn whether the robbers would strike this trip.

Landrum was snoring fitfully. Wye decided to check the express car. He went down the aisle to the rear of the coach and stepped across to the express-baggage, whose door was unlocked. The three guards gave him alert stares; each of them was armed with a shotgun as well as rifle and handgun.

Wye said, "Everything all right?"

"Silky as old bourbon," said the oldest guard, a stocky and grizzled man named Mort Zander. The air was dim and

65

reeking with cigarette smoke; Wye eased over to a drafty window which dissipated the acrid bite of fumes, saying agreeably, "It's close in here."

"Yeah. We got to keep her locked all around, though, 'cept from your car. Orders."

"You worry too much," yawned a lantern-jawed young guard. "I made three runs on this duty and didn't get hit a time. Always carry a charm." He pulled a pint bottle out of his jacket. "Anybody want a snort of her?"

"No." Wye's glance turned; his face was hard and smooth. "Neither do you. Put it away."

Starting to yank the cork with his teeth, the young man lifted a wicked stare. "Who'll make me?"

Zander said, "All right, Pete."

"All right, hell." Pete was lounging to his feet. "We take our pay and our orders from Old Man Fancher, not this goddamn bluenose. Why you sticking up for a goddamn bluenose, Mort?"

"I ain't. You could just land us all in a jackpot of trouble by drinking, son. Ease down."

"Jesus," said the third guard, who was crowded against a window at the front of the car. "Is that an army?"

The train was slowing perceptibly as it lunged into the last yards of a long climbing grade. Wye moved up swiftly beside the guard; so did Mort and Pete. At the summit of the incline, standing against the sky, a large group of men and horses waited by the track. Pete said softly, "Son of a bitch. Will you look at that?" Mort said nothing; the rhythm of his jaw working a tobacco cud did not break, but he carefully eared back the hammers of his shotgun.

Wye left them and returned to the passenger coach. He put a hand on Landrum's shoulder and shook him awake. The sheriff said fumblingly, "What the hell," and Wye pointed. Landrum pressed his face against the window and said, "My God." He scooped up the rifle he had leaned against his knee.

They had picked a place for it, Wye thought grimly; the train had labored into a slowing rate of climb that was becoming more and more pronounced, and the riders had placed themselves at the peak of the ascent. By now, though, Wye was getting a closer sight of them, and he was

66

puzzled. There was no sign of the shapeless slickers, black hats and mask always worn by the robbers. Though the riders were heavily armed, their weapons remained sheathed; some were standing quietly by their horses, others squatted on their haunches, smoking and talking. And now one of them, a towering man in black, had come over to the track and was flagging the train with a red bandanna.

"Well, by Christ, it's McKelvey," Landrum burst out. "We better get word up to the cab to old Fletcher."

"No need. He's slowing her now."

The brakes whistled and shrieked; a clank of couplings ran the length of the train. Wye was dropping off on the roadbed before the cars had ground to a halt. McKelvey had turned to his men and was rapping orders as Wye came up to him.

"Glad you made it," Wye told him. "What delayed these fellows, anyway?"

"No delay." McKelvey neatly folded the bandanna and tucked it in his pocket. "Never was. But I wanted all of you to think there was." He gave Landrum a nod as the sheriff plodded over, his face slack with perplexity. "It seemed wisest, seeing as I didn't know who to trust."

Wye nodded his understanding. "You didn't want your men seen boarding the train in Leedstock."

"Exactly. I had the St. Louis office dispatch a force of men to Repville; they were waiting for me there. I know these mountains like my hand—no problem to lead 'em up here over an old trail I know. We haven't been here over two hours. We're just short of the stretch where the trains are always hit. This time that bunch will run into something they never expected. A small army."

"You seem almighty sure they'll hit," Landrum said in a cranky tone.

McKelvey said with a grim certainty, "They will," and turned back to his men, barking a few more commands. A wood ramp was lifted down from one of the freight cars, and the detectives drove their horses up it to fill one car, then the other. Afterward they fanned out swiftly and efficiently across the train, some of them joining the three guards in the express car, others being stationed in the freight cars and the caboose, and the rest seating themselves in the passenger

67

coach. McKelvey went up front to speak to the engineer; he checked the train from engine to caboose, and finally joined Wye in the coach as the train started up again.

"Well, that's it." The old detective took off his hat and ran a hand back over his silvery hair. "Now all we do is wait."

"Having those two empty cars attached was your idea?"

McKelvey nodded. "I arranged it with the railroad boys on the Repville end. We'll likely need the horses again before this is over."

"There's just one thing. How can you be sure that Dundie will try for this particular train?"

McKelvey gave him a bloodless glance. "You're not required to know. Suffice it to say that I not only have assurance that Dundie knows about today's shipment and its worth, I know the exact place where he'll try to seize it."

"Look," Wye said angrily, "you're supposed to be cooperating with our office. O. K., your trap is set and it's safe to tell me now even if you don't trust me. How could you know?"

McKelvey said, "All in good time," and his eyes were impervious. He clamped his jaw as if shutting it against further talk.

Wye put down the rising simmer of his temper because it would get him nowhere. He couldn't help wondering if McKelvey's close-mouthed manner had anything to do with his trip up to Dundie's town—where, as he'd claimed, he had found no trace of Poe Lockhart. He'd been oddly evasive about that business too, or so it had seemed to Wye.

Wye tried to doze some more as the train roared and rattled deeper into the high country. Finally he rose to stretch his legs, walking up to the front of the car. Wye nodded to a pair of detectives quietly talking there, and peered out the window. The train was curving gently around a vast squashed cone of a mountain, the roadbed burrowing low along its flank; monstrous cliffs and escarpments soared brokenly on every side, straggling fingers of pine darkening their granite-gray slopes. A fine mist of rain or rain-heavy fog was drifting across the mountainsides, slowly hazing the panorama into a woolly obscurity. The roadbed began to straighten, and was gradually snaking onto a wide plateau.

One of the detectives across from Wye took a cigar from

his mouth as he answered his companion's question, at the same time glancing through the window. He said, "Holy Jesus," and dropped the cigar. "A barricade!"

Wye went across the aisle and looked out this side, where the inward curve of roadbed gave him a view of the tracks ahead. From beyond a turn, a jumble of logs and rocks piled across the tracks had come suddenly into view. The engineer applied the brakes; the drag on the cars' momentum was swift, but the brakes seemed ready to burn out, and the barricade was rushing toward them.

The cowcatcher slammed into the pile and scattered wood and rubble to either side, and the train went bucking past the spot still holding the rails. The cars were slowing rapidly, brakes screaming. "Drop down!" McKelvey roared. "Brace yourselves!" The detectives flattened against the seats as the train jarred and crashed to a whole stop.

Even as they stumbled back to their feet, Wye could see men materializing out of the heavy brush flanking the roadbed—men in slickers and black hats and bandanna masks. Even in this confused instant, it was clear how neatly the thing had been staged. The bandits had placed themselves precisely; no time was wasted fanning out, and they were swarming across the train already. Some would be at the engineer and fireman and likely flooding the firebox; others were covering the caboose, the express and passenger cars.

The first bandit into the coach lunged through the vestibule, gun in hand; he braced to a stop as he saw the number of men inside. He shouted hoarsely and opened fire. A detective rolled out of his seat to the floor, hugging his belly. The outlaw spun belatedly for the door then; three shots drove into his back, and he plunged into the vestibule, dead before he hit the floor.

A second outlaw bawled, "A trap, a trap," as he dropped back to the roadside. There was a hanging fragment of silence as if the mind of each individual, outlaw or detective, were making a tiny screw-turn of adjustment to fix tightly on the situation facing them all. A few seconds later the stillness dissolved in the rattle of gunfire mingled with men's curses and a sound of glass shattering as the detectives opened up from the windows and the men outside returned the fusillade.

69

The outlaws broke into full retreat, firing as they went backward into the brush and plunged down a dropaway slope that cut them off at once from the train. Wye and Clete Landrum were among the first to spill off the train in pursuit. A reek of powdersmoke mingled with the foggy rain. Above the melee of shots and yells, McKelvey was calling orders that might or might not be obeyed; every man was on his own now. The detectives were laying a raking fire on the long slope to chop down the outlaws as they ran toward the bottom where scrub pine and dense brush offered a plentiful cover.

Now a few detectives cut down the open slope in reckless pursuit. Wye took the fever too, but Clete Landrum, cool-voiced now, caught his arm. "Our job's to see after the gold. Few of 'em reached the express car. Come on!"

They wheeled back through a fringe of brush toward the train. A torrent of smoke gushing from a caboose hotbox was bannering like a black curtain past the express car, but as they broke out of the brush, the wind changed; the air cleared. They saw that three outlaws with more daring than good sense had decided on a last-ditch try for the gold, and they were pouring a barrage of shots into the express car. The guards were holding their own.

Landrum yelled, "Throw down your guns!"

Their answer was to turn their guns on the two lawmen. Wye fired back and a man went down. Landrum's buffalo rifle bellowed like a young cannon, slamming a second outlaw off his feet and flinging him across the gravel like a broken doll. The third man kept doggedly shooting. Landrum grunted and folded up slowly, grabbing his middle. Another bullet struck him.

Wye dropped to his knee to steady his aim on the third man who was pivoting away toward the brush. His foot slipped on the rain-slick gravel and he fell, but at once rolled in a catlike recovery to his feet, his mask slipping down.

Wye's hand froze around his gun, a cry choking back in his throat. Gil hesitated, his pistol half-lifted, staring at his brother; again he swung about and this time was quickly swallowed by the brush.

Wye came unsteadily to his feet. The excitement and rage had run out of his belly; he felt like a gutted man. He stooped beside Clete Landrum and rolled him on his back.

70

Clete's body was inert and loose, and the second bullet had taken him in the face.

The mist thickening into a soft rain blew across Wye's face like a clammy hand. He looked at the outlaw groaning on the ground a few yards away, hip broken by Wye's shot, and did not see the man at all. *Gil,* he thought sickly.

CHAPTER ELEVEN

Even Poe Lockhart had been stunned by the effectiveness of the trap he'd helped set for Dundie's men. He had seen at least four of them go down, and even then the pale anonymity of the rain-dense fog had masked most of the action. Now as he and the other holdup men retreated down the long slope that began below the roadbed, he threw back a few token shots at the pursuers, careful to hold his fire high. Actually a man could make out almost nothing beyond thirty yards; and in a minute he and the others were deep in the trees and brush below the slope, and some of the detectives weren't far behind.

There were thrashings, yells, vagrant shots all around him in the gray murk as Poe pressed cautiously along, his gun out. He had tried desperately to keep track of Gil, but because of the fog he'd lost sight of his son at the outset. Gil was out there somewhere: cut down at the first volley, dead or wounded, maybe lost in the fog, or possibly finding his way back to the motte of cottonwoods where Dundie's men had left their horses. There was no way of telling what had really happened to him, and the sick worry balled in Poe's guts with an icy and paralyzing force.

All he could do was strike back directly toward the motte and the horses—and hope. Though he was in a hurry, Poe did not plunge ahead blindly; his ears, trained to acuteness by years in the twilight world of Coldrock, ferreted out each sound that reached him, weighing and cataloging it to guide his movements. Clinging always to heavy cover, moving like an Indian, he deftly avoided contact with men he could

71

make out to the left and right of him. Soon the noises were falling behind, and now he moved boldly in a straight swift line toward the motte.

Poe reached the trees as a pair of yellow-slickered riders bolted out, straining low to their horses' necks. He yelled at them but both men were intent on escape, and they tore away into the brush. Poe dived through the grove, shouting Gil's name. He saw a number of horses still tied here, among them Gil's and his own. He pushed grim-jawed among the restless animals and left the motte, heading back toward the melee he had just left behind him.

While they had been laying up to wait for the train, old habit had prompted him to commit as much of the terrain as possible to memory. Recalling now that they had crossed a dry wash which twisted back through the brush in the direction he was moving, he quickly looked for it: the high banks would offer some shelter, and he could move quickly along its brush-free bottom.

Locating the old barranca almost at once, Poe dropped down the bank. At the bottom he wheeled, his gun ready, as two figures came stumbling up through the fog. He quickly recognized two of the gang, the Barrows brothers, Lank and Ed. They were mulattoes, beanpoles of men with long horse faces. Lank was supporting his brother.

"Ed got hit." The bony planes of Lank's face gleamed wetly. "We got to get out of here. You going the wrong way, man."

Poe grabbed his arm. "You see Gil back there?"

"Man, I think your boy, he get caught for fair. I see him came a-raring off the tracks like the devil was behind him. Him and a couple others, they tried for the express car. Goddamn fools, them. I think they all got cut down but your boy, but it looked to me like some of them Johnny Laws spotted him and was sewing him up. I was too busy running to tell, can't tell nothing for sure in this damn soup." Lank rubbed a hand over his wet face. "Jesus, man. They's an army of 'em. They a-cutting us down like flies. I think they got Clem. He was hit, and I see him go down."

Poe was already pounding away down the wash, and Lank called after him, "You crazy going back there, man."

Again now Poe could make out the tight, small noises of danger on every side; he was back in the thick of it and had to go carefully. The shooting had slacked off, but he knew that the detectives were beating warily about through the brush to flush out any stray outlaws. Some of the gangmen, he supposed, would have lost their bearings in the fog and be unable to find the horses.

What about Gil? And would he give up if the detectives cornered him? Poe knew the answer at once: he wouldn't have given up at Gil's age, and neither would his son.

A panic thickened Poe's throat; there was only a blind thin chance of finding his son now, but he had to try. There was still a half-concentrated burst of sporadic shooting at one point up ahead and near the tracks, and remembering what Lank had said about the detectives probably sewing Gil up, he thought, *As good a place as any to try—get over there.*

Poe came to a dead halt as a man rose darkly out of the thickets at the top of one bank. "Who is it?" the man said hoarsely. The barrel of his rifle, leveled on Poe's heart, glistened in the mist. His voice did not belong to a gangman. He must have posted himself here to intercept any outlaws who fled down the wash; but Poe had come from the other direction, and this accounted for the puzzled uncertainty in his tone.

Poe said quietly, "It's me, you damned fool. Take it easy." He scaled the bank, his heels driving at the gravel. The man was saying hesitantly, "You wait. I don't"— as Poe batted the rifle aside with his palm, at the same time chopping his pistol across the man's jaw. The detective sank down without a sound.

Poe bent and scooped up the rifle, then stepped over his prone form and slammed off left through the bushes, heedless of the raking branches. He paused just once to get his bearings, afterward angling toward that sound of heavy firing below the tracks. Ahead now he made out the shape of a high granite abutment he had mentally charted earlier, and he thought the shooting was coming from just beyond it.

Hugging its flinty roughness, Poe climbed the abutment and flattened along its top. Through the heavy mistlike rain he saw the orange tongues of gunflame that showed at least three men laid up in good cover in a cluster of massive rocks while they poured a steady fire at an isolated boulder where one man was pinned, shooting back doggedly. It took Poe a

73

good half-minute to pick out all the details available in this wet dimness, and by then he'd identified the man behind the rock by the white-spotted red bandanna mask, damp-dark and limp now against his yellow slicker. This was Gil, and Poe hesitated no longer.

Working the rifle as fast as he could, he laid down a close fire around the three detectives. He was above them and he had a clean view. His gunflashes offered the only target, and this wasn't enough to keep one of the men from quitting abruptly: he left the boulders and sprinted away into the brush. A second man followed him. The third detective held his ground, pumping shots alternately at Poe's position and at Gil's. Poe fired so near the detective that splinters of rock showered over and around him, but still he stood fast.

Gil could not break out of the trap while this man's rifle was waiting, and at any moment the other two might return with reinforcements. Poe cupped his hands to his mouth.

"Gil!" he roared. "You hear me?"

There was a pause, then Gil's voice rose, faintly excited with relief. "I hear you, Pa."

"When I shoot again, break and run over here . . . I'll be covering you."

Because there was no other way, Poe pulled a careful bead on the protruding leg of the man below, and pulled trigger. The detective howled and cramped himself tighter into the boulders, gripping his hit leg. Gil broke away from his shelter and came on a zigzag run for the abutment. Poe lent him a brief covering fire, and then abruptly his magazine was empty.

Gil had covered most of the distance when the detective fired. Gil crumpled down, his momentum somersaulting him on his back. Poe's heart seemed to clot in his throat, but Gil was up almost at once, running again, though in a dazed and labored way. Then he was behind the abutment. "Pa?"

Poe inched backward off the rock and dropped to the ground beside him. There was a wet dark smear along his temple under the crush-crowned black hat, no more than a nick. Poe snapped, "This way," and caught Gil's arm and hurried him toward the wash. The two of them floundered down its stony bank and pushed along the bottom at a slow trot. A faintness of voices and crackling brush reached

74

them: the seraching men were on every side, and they could be spotted at any moment.

"Pa," Gil hissed between his teeth. "Some bastard give us away, how the whole thing was set up. Some bastard . . ."

Poe said, "Save it," and he toyed with the impulse to try locating McKelvey and surrendering himself and Gil as had been originally planned at their final meeting when he'd fully appraised McKelvey of the intended raid today. McKelvey would be out there among the searchers, but a cold danger lay in attempting any sort of contact in this rainy fog that hid a man's identity beyond a few yards' distance. Even if McKelvey had warned his men that Poe Lockhart was on their side, few or none of these men would know him. Raw-nerved in this mist where individuals were only dim shadows, McKelvey's men had already, he was sure, wasted a good many of the shots he'd heard in firing blindly at anything that moved or made a noise. Nevertheless, Poe would have taken the gamble and called out except for knowing that Gil would react to the betrayal like a wildcat, and taking on a son his own size and twenty-odd years younger, wasn't to Poe's taste.

Not yet, he cautioned himself. *Just bide your time and watch your chance.* For now he would go along with the escape: keeping Gil alive was his first concern. At least the gang was broken to pieces and the depredations on Fancher's gold trains ended; he had fulfilled his part of the bargain, and he was sure McKelvey would keep his part. It was only a question of when and how to get to him with Gil in tow and without getting cut down by McKelvey's men.

They approached the motte with care. The detectives would be looking for the horses in order to keep the quarry afoot, and Poe had half-expected the motte to be discovered by now. To his relief he found at least half the horses still tethered there. That first salvo at the train must have taken a heavy toll of the gang, otherwise most of them would have broken away by now.

Poe and Gil flung themselves into the saddles and reined out of the motte as several detectives came bursting through a wall of brush only yards away, firing as they came. Poe spurred sidelong, veering into the thickets, and Gil was on his heels. On foot, the detectives were left quickly behind.

Shortly, feeling his way by instinct through the fog, Poe

guided them into a narrow canyon, the first leg of their escape route. This was a familiar pattern to him. Years ago he had planned every detail of his holdups with exquisite care, and Clem Dundie had improved on his methods, Poe thought with a certain professional admiration.

The horses that the gang used on jobs were all solid color or typically marked; none had distinctive markings, and they were kept in a remote valley pocketed back in the hills. They were equipped with special saddles kept nearby, along with the slickers and hats and boots worn as disguises, in the same high country cave where the looted gold was cached. Yesterday each horse had been put through a careful set of paces: a three-mile running dash, then a half-mile at a trot, and a half-mile at a walk, alternated by short running spurts.

The men had reached the holdup site on three separate trails, but not as groups; they stayed well apart in order to discipline themselves for the escape, when each man would be on his own on these trails which were laid out to provide doublebacks, passages through creeks and across bare rock and down washes floored with loose sand. If one man were seen and fired on, the others would be isolated enough to scatter and get away. They would drift back into Jenny Camp at odd times over the next couple of days; men came and went at will in the town, so that it would be impossible to keep track of any single man and match his movements to the robbery, if the law cared to try.

This time, of course, the usual procedure would be abandoned; there would be no returning to Jenny Camp by those who'd escaped the trap. McKelvey would be sending men to clean out the town and burn it to the ground; he had told Poe as much. Dundie, always coppering his bets, had told them just before the holdup where they would meet if something went wrong: some caves well back in the peaks. Poe had only a vague notion of the location, but Gil had been there once.

They would hold to the original escape route only until they were certain any pursuit was shaken; afterward they would strike out for the caves.

They moved at an easy gait, taking only mechanical precautions; there was little need for haste or care now, for the rain had thickened to a steady, pelting downpour that

76

would quickly wipe any track clean. They rode into a stretch of pine woods where the force of the rain was broken; Gil rode with his head down, his bandanna pressed to his temple.

Poe said, "You all right?"

"Just a crease," Gil said. His voice was strong, but there was an underlying dullness that Poe didn't miss. "That sonofabitching inside man of Clem's," Gil muttered. "Crossed us all for sure. Had to be him."

Poe said idly, "Seems to me I never did hear who he was."

"Hell, none of us know," Gil said disgustedly. "Clem always met him in secret. Had to be him for sure. Goddamn, if I had his name . . ."

Poe didn't answer. They had been on the trail for some minutes, and had seen nobody else. By now, he was thinking, things would have simmered down back by the train, and McKelvey would be collecting his prisoners and counting the dead. This was the time, with the nervous excitement passed, to turn back and give up himself and Gil. But how to take his son with him? If he put a gun on the boy, he'd almost certainly be forced to use it. It had taken too many years for Poe to tamp down his own Lockhart wildness for him to reserve much doubt on that score.

Only if he were physically helpless could Gil be taken back alive: Poe would have to buffalo him solidly and put him out cold with the first blow. The idea worried him, particularly with Gil wearing a head wound already, but there was no other way. He dropped slightly behind his son, pushing back the skirt of his slicker.

Gil said without turning his head, "Pa."

Poe eased the half-drawn pistol back in its holster, saying woodenly, "What?"

"I killed a man by the train."

The horses plodded slowly out of the pine forest, their hoofs muffled by the thick needle-loam. A gust of rainy wind rode freshly against Poe's face and body, but it wasn't this that made him grow cold, deep cold to the guts of him. The seconds ran together and still Gil did not look around, and Poe, not wanting to meet his son's eyes just then, was glad.

Gil said at last, softly, "Pa, you hear what I said?"

77

"Know his name?"

"Sheriff"— Gil paused, clearing his throat. "It was Sheriff Landrum."

"Jesus God," Poe said very quietly. "You didn't pick your fish undersize, did you, boy?"

"There wasn't no other way. Me and Clint and Murph went after the express car, and him and Wye come up. He got Murph with this goddamn buffalo gun, and Wye busted Clint in the leg. So I shot back. He—"

Poe said in a clipped tense way, "Was Wye hurt?"

"No. But he seen my face, Pa—Wye did. Mask slipped and he got a clear look at me for sure."

"Chance you didn't get Landrum cold."

Gil shook his head dismally. "Pa, I got him cold. You seen the way he fell, you'd of believed it."

Poe said with no real hope, "No allowing that Wye might cover you, you reckon?"

Gli laughed bitterly; he hammered a fist against his pommel. "Not a lone chance he won't tell, you can lay to that. Even if it means he'll have to wear a killer brother around his neck for the world to see, he won't. That's the way he is."

They rocked in their saddles in silence for a full two minutes, the rain bucketing in chilly plummets across their huddled bodies; and Poe said at last, "What's done is done. Right now we better worry about finding the others."

For that was how it had to be now. However far McKelvey might stretch his connections to keep his bargain of softened prison terms for them both, even he could not— and would not, Poe knew—let the bargain cover the willful killing of a law officer. And that left no alternative but to find a sanctuary of sorts with the broken remainder of Dundie's gang and lay low while the country was turned inside out in the search for Landrum's killer. No alternative, that was, except to take his son in to face a hangman's noose.

CHAPTER TWELVE

It had rained off and on for two days; today was sunny, and the air was clean-washed. Small Benny was making mud pies in the yard while Margaret Chaney, seated in the porch swing, kept a watchful eye on him to make sure he didn't get too dirty. Ben Yarbrough stood on the porch, leaning his shoulder against a gallery post as he watched the gig-turn up the long curving lane toward the Talon ranchhouse.

Benny leaped up, crying, "Grand'pa, Gran'pa," as he ran to the gate.

"Benny!" Margaret laid her knitting aside and came over beside Ben Yarbrough. She was a slender, graying woman in her late forties who had kept house for Yarbrough and been a nursemaid to Benny since Emmaline's death. "Don't smile," she told him tartly. "You son has already skinned both knees this morning from running so."

"Why, that's in the nature of boyhood, Margaret."

Benjy pulled the bays up smartly; Barrett Fancher descended from the gig and scooped the boy up in his arms. He was always brisk, but usually brusque too; today he seemed unusually jaunty. He had good cause to be, with Dundie's depredations ended, his gang all but wiped out, and Jenny Camp burned to the ground. Several of the gang, glad to exchange what they knew for a lighter prison sentence, had betrayed the location of the cave where the stolen gold had been stored. A pleasant surprise for Barrett Fancher, who had written that gold off as a loss.

Fancher came to the porch carrying Benny on one arm; he tipped his hat. "Morning, Miss Chaney—Ben. Thought I might take the lad for a short ride."

"Wait, just a minute," Margaret said. "The sun is fierce today, I'll get a cap for him." She went into the house.

"Pity about Clete Landrum." Fancher soberly flicked ash

79

from his cigar. "Feel badly because it was my gold he died defending. In a few months he'd have been out of office and established in a nice, safe storekeeper's rut. And only last week we'd made a long-term loan to get him started. Too bad."

Yarbrough said, "How is his daughter taking it?"

"A brutal time for her. Luckily there's Wye to comfort her. And I'm seeing that she lacks for nothing till she's decided what she'll do next."

"In any case, it'll likely force her decision about Wye," Yarbrough observed. "You know he's been asking Tacey to marry him for weeks."

Fancher nodded, a preoccupied frown knitting his brows. "Wye's been acting strangely of late. Moody and distant—even a bit sharp with his friends. Have you noticed?"

"No, but I haven't seen him since Clete's funeral." Ben paused. "Come to think, he did seem pretty distraught, but I put it down to the way Clete died. Wye saw him shot down, and they were close you know."

Fancher shook his head slowly. "I think there's more to account, Ben."

"Well, he's acting sheriff now, and he could be fretful about doing his best and giving the body politic something to vote for this fall."

"That could be part of it—in the sense that as sheriff, he's sending out men who could hunt down and kill his brother. Gil's among those still at large if, as we may assume, he was with the robbers. And oddly, in spite of everything, Wye and Gil were always close enough."

"Blood's still thicker than vinegar," Yarbrough agreed half-absently. "Pity Dundie and those others got away. Have the posses found anything?"

"They've rounded up a few, and of course McKelvey's still on the job, though he's sent all but a few of his men back to St. Louis. I asked him to stay till Dundie himself is taken—I won't feel easy in my bones till he is. Meantime I've announced a reward of two thousand dollars for information leading to his capture, and another two thousand to whoever can pinpoint the outlaw that killed Clete Landrum. That ought to get results." Fancher drew gently on his cigar, eyes narrowed against the furling smoke.

"I'd give a prettier penny yet to know how Dundie obtained his information on our shipments—and through whom. If it could be done once, it could be done again."

"Not by Dundie, anyway," Yarbrough smiled. "His men who were captured have spilled enough to get him twenty years if he's caught. He'll either have to lie low and head back to Mexico if he hasn't already done so—and with the handful of men he'll have left, he has little choice."

"That's true. Well—"

Benny had been toying with his grandfather's watch chain; losing interest now, he wriggled impatiently. "I wanna go for a ride, Gran'pa. Daddy?"

"All right, son, as soon as Margaret—here she comes."

Margaret fitted a broad-billed cap on Benny's curls, saying crisply, "Not too long, Mr. Fancher. He's sensitive to sunlight."

Fancher looked faintly sardonic. "It seems to me, ma'am, that lack of exercise, sun, and fresh air is what's largely responsible for his condition. Bit of roughnecking never hurt any boy. He should be learning how to ride and shoot and swim."

A flush stained Margaret's cheeks. "He's only four, sir."

"He's old enough to walk, ma'am." Fancher carried the boy across the yard and swung him up to the gig's seat. "Now let's raise a little dust, boy, eh? The north road, Benjamin."

The gig swung around and rolled down the lane. Margaret shaded her eyes, gazing after it. Yarbrough smiled, "Margaret, you're a regular brood hen."

"Benny is not well," she said tautly. "And he sunburns much too easily."

"So did I as a kid," Yarbrough said good-humoredly. "Fair-complected boys generally do. They need toughening."

Behind the easy surface of his words, as he stared after the handsome gig and the high-stepping bays, an old, familiar bitterness was hardening like a knotted muscle in Ben Yarbrough's guts.

As a young man he had dreamed of fortune; he was no longer young, and he was far from rich. The ranch and the bone of a banker's job Fancher had tossed him totaled up to

81

a middling success, no more. Yarbrough might have mellowed into acceptance of his limitations except for a constant awareness of the vast sums that Barrett Fancher juggled daily in his many transactions. Nearly every day of his life, Yarbrough saw and handled a large part of the Fancher fortune, and so his bitterness was a daily, growing thing. Fancher, he remembered, had been a millionaire at his age.

Yarbrough's fist gently clenched and unclenched at his side. The old man's will was so set up that he would never be able to touch a cent of the fortune his son would inherit, and even if he could, Barrett Fancher seemed in a fair way to see a very ripe old age. Meantime the money was there, more money than one man had a right to—if there were only a way to separate him from some of it.

And then it came to him like a thunderclap. Of course . . . *Benny*.

His son was the apple of his Grandfather Fancher's eye. Suddenly the way was clear before Yarbrough, even the details of the idea swarming through his mind all at once. He had the odd feeling that the notion had been there all along, like a waiting seed not quite permitted to be nourished.

To bring it off, he would need to take a deadly risk, and this knowledge gave Yarbrough pause. But a cold, reckless excitement was gripping him now; the stakes were worth the risk. Two hours from now he could be dead—or he would have the key to a fortune in his fist.

Drawing out his watch, Yarbrough checked it; his lips thinned. There was no time to lose. "Margaret," he cleared his throat with authority—"Mr. Fancher was right, I think. Benny needs to spend more time out of doors. Seeing that he does will be your job."

"Why—certainly, if that's what—"

"In fact I want him to spend as much of each day as he pleases outside, weather allowing. And I want you to take him on daily walks, a little farther each day. And we'll start him out on a gentle horse, leading him around the corral. I'll assign one of the crew to help you with that. Understood?"

"Just as you wish."

His brusqueness had turned her manner cool, but

Yarbrough hardly noticed as he added that he had business in town and might not be back in time for supper.

In ten minutes he was riding away from Talon on the town road, but once out of sight of the headquarters he struck off northeast toward the foothills. He set his horse to a brisk but not hurried clip; he would reach the rendezvous barely in time, but that would be soon enough. There was a wry twist to the urgency he felt; only a short hour ago he'd had no intention whatever of showing up at today's meeting. After all, his last rendezvous with Dundie had been a week ago, a full three days before the unexpected trap that had cut Dundie's gang to pieces.

At that time, they had arranged to meet today at the usual place, but Yarbrough had decided after the aborted robbery that he'd be wise to quietly drop his connection with the outlaw leader as of now. It wasn't only that Dundie was now a hunted man, his gang all but wiped out, and therefore of no use to Yarbrough—it was also that Dundie would have questions that would be hard to answer. Somebody had surely betrayed him, and his first suspicion would naturally lock on his "inside man."

Now Yarbrough ran his mind over the likely range of those questions, answering each in a careful detail to his own satisfaction. But his belly was tight with the knowledge that the only one he needed to satisfy was Clem Dundie—and Dundie would be in a killing mood.

Yarbrough met the climbing timber of the foothills and moved high into it, and came onto a bare ridge where he paused to let his horse blow while he took the idle precaution of scanning his backtrail. Afterward he moved on deeper into the hills, and came finally to the mouth of a small canyon. A stream with grassy banks ran through the cleft, and Yarbrough rode along it. The canyon widened gradually and its bald gray walls gained an easy slant.

Yarbrough halted at last by a chunk of fallen rimrock and dismounted, leading his horse to the edge of the roiling stream. This put his back to one of the slanting walls, and he thought, *Ten to one he's watching from up there.* He let his horse dip its muzzle in the water and drink, making all his movements casual. Yet a chill chased down his spine; he could almost feel a watcher's eyes. Even when he heard a

83

grate of boots as a man descended the wall behind him, Yarbrough did not turn, only remarked, "There ought to be trout in here."

Dundie said, "I didn't think you'd show," his tone soft and measured and wicked.

Yarbrough said laconically, "Neither did I," and turned on his heel to face the outlaw leader. Dundie had his pistol out and leveled. He was bareheaded, the twist of cloth around his scalp discolored by the same rusty stains that caked the dirty bandanna knotted around his wrist. Usually immaculate, he had a raw, unshaven look; his eyes were the color of thin pond ice.

"I'll bet," Yarbrough said mildly, "you're curious to know how it was a whole gang of Parkinsons was waiting for you."

"By God, don't play games with me!" Dundie's voice was electric with crackling rage. "They broke up my men— captured or killed, most of them. They reduced both Jenny Camp and our cabins to ashes. They found the cave where we'd cached the gold."

"Somebody talked. But you don't know who, I take it."

"That," Dundie said softly, "is all that kept me from pulling the trigger the moment you crossed my sights."

"You're all in a lather." Yarbrough planted one fist on his hip and cuffed back his hat on his sweaty hair. "Be as lathered as you want, but while you're about it, consider that to date I've tipped you off to half a dozen good-sized shipments, everything from train time to the number of guards and how they'd be armed and disposed. If I was setting up a trap for you, I waited mighty long to spring it. And what would there be in it for me but a jail term if I made it known I was your inside boy? On top of that, a fat piece of the hauls I had coming has been lost to me. Stop and think."

"I am thinking." Dundie continued to eye him wickedly. "I'm thinking it was you who first came to me up in Jenny Camp and offered your services. I'm also thinking that a belated qualm of conscience might prod a man to almost anything. Also that since Fancher has one jailbird son-in-law in Poe Lockhart, he might not hanker to double that disgrace—that if you'd gone to him, made a clean breast and informed on us, he'd be inclined to forgive and forget."

Yarbrough smiled with a confidence he did not yet feel. "That has a pretty thin sound, I think you'll admit. Besides I took a long chance in coming here today, knowing how you'd feel."

"Man, if you're the one who set up a trap to snare me and that part of it failed, stands to reason ye'd be asked to carry on the deception a bit longer." But Dundie had lowered his pistol, and Yarbrough held in a sigh of relief; he knew that Dundie was more than half-convinced that his betrayer wasn't Ben Yarbrough.

"Well, I don't blame a man for being careful," Yarbrough said, and added idly, "Who's your newest man? Poe Lockhart?"

"I've considered him," Dundie said, and shook his head. "I don't think so. There's damned little honor among men, thieves or otherwise—but it's a man's reasons that I closely scan. Poe broke prison and killed the man sent after him— and McKelvey took his life in his hands when he pulled a gun on Poe in Alabam's place. All that rings true enough."

Yarbrough settled down on his haunches and plucked a grass stem; he bit off the tip. "You know, he and McKelvey could have arranged all that weeks ago. Even his prison break could have been faked, and a false story given out about his killing Tom Rydell."

"Damn it," Dundie said savagely, "never tell me what a man *might* do unless ye back it with reason! Why would he cooperate with the law and help lay a trap that could have gotten his boy Gil killed?"

"Perhaps," Yarbrough murmured, "because he agreed to work with the authorities in exchange for a lightened sentence—he still had time to serve. And he might have readily preferred to take a chance with Gil's life than see him branded an outlaw. If Gil were captured now, he'd face only a couple years in prison."

Dundie walked a short circle, kicking at the ground with a restless tensile energy. "Poe's changed, all right," he muttered. "A change not quite definable, yet it's there. And that day McKelvey came and I had Poe escort him out of Jenny Camp—they could have talked then and set things up. And several chances to give away the game, if he were doing so."

"Well, of course we can't be sure of anything."

85

Yarbrough almost smiled; it would be better at this point to let Dundie convince himself. "What are your plans for the future?"

"Plans—what plans d'ye think I could have now?" A fresh suspicion stung Dundie's pale eyes. "Why d'ye ask?"

Yarbrough's reply was oblique. "As I see it, you have two choices. Return to Mexico with empty pockets or with full ones."

Dundie snapped, "There's no choice that I see. At least one of my men who was taken told the law everything, and thanks to the sheriff getting himself killed, it'll mean my scalp if I'm caught. And what in the hell can I do with the handful of men left me?"

Yarbrough grinned. "A handful will be best for what I have in mind, and the money will split fewer ways. More money than you'd see in a year of robbing Fancher's gold trains. Sure money, my friend, for one soft and easy job. Are you listening?"

A little grudgingly, Dundie nodded.

CHAPTER THIRTEEN

Squatting in the cave's mouth, the gang wolfed their meager supper. The food was cold; all the cooking had to be done at night with the fire hidden in a brush-flanked hollow. And now Lank Barrows had returned from Leedstock without the grub supplies he'd been sent to buy. Lank had been chosen for the errand because he was an anonymous scarecrow of a man with a mild, inoffensive manner, his face almost unknown to the law. Everybody left of the gang was present except Pima Jack, who was standing his usual daylight guard on a ridge that commanded the valley approaches to this narrow, brush-grown plateau deep in the peaks. The face of the giant, looming ridge was honeycombed with caverns.

Lank said, "I dropped in at the saloon like you wanted me to—for what-all I could hear, Clem." Sitting on his lean

86

shanks, he sucked thick black coffee from a soot-charred cup, straining out the grounds through his teeth. "I hadn't asked only a few questions when he come in. Ol' McKelvey himself. He ordered a drink and just stood there, but I tell you, man, it give me deep-down shivers, way he looked at me."

Squatting on his heels with a blanket huddled around his shoulders, Dundie scowled. He was in an evil humor because yesterday the weather had turned foul again, and he'd come down with fever and chills during the night. "I hope you didn't give anything away to Boiler Britches, Lank."

"No sir, man, I was careful. I had another drink and didn't clear out too quick. But that old man had his eye on me; didn't figure I'd best be seen riding out of town with a pack of grub."

Dundie said curtly, "That's right," his voice dissolving into a wracking cough.

"Pretty soon we need food," Smoky put in. "There is no more flour. On'y a little bacon and some cans of tomatoes. The coffee is 'mos' gone."

She sat cross-legged beside Gil; they were sharing the last of the biscuits and cold beef. All the girls of Jenny Camp but Smoky had quietly left the country after the detectives had herded them out, permitting them only a few minutes to collect their few belongings before the town was put to the torch. No charges were brought against the women, and with their soft and lazy life in the outlaw camp gone up in smoke, they had no reason to stay. None of them, that was, but Smoky; she had guessed where the gang members would rendezvous and had come on foot to join Gil at the caves. The men were more than satisfied to have somebody about to do the cooking.

"Son of a bitch," Dandy Mack McMurdo said in a quiet and vicious way. "My belly is wrapping around my backbone as it is."

Dundie speared a tomato from the can he held and put it in his mouth, then motioned at Lank with the knife. "You said you asked a few questions. What manner of answers did ye get?"

Barrows shifted on his haunches. "Well, the posses of local folk have pretty much quit the search. They was

87

disgusted by the bad weather and by not picking up any sign of you. Ony thing kept them on the hunt so long was that Sheriff Landrum was a mighty well-liked man."

"That's so." A raw nerve was touched in Dundie; his wrath was up again. "So long as there was no killing, the locals were more pleased by our activities than otherwise, seeing it was Barrett Fancher's pocket we were picking. Now the countryside is up in arms. By God, if I should learn what fool shot Landrum, he'll be lucky if the locals find him first."

Poe noticed a fragmentary pause of Gil's hand as it lifted a cup to his lips; then he tilted it and drank. They'd agreed between them that no good would be served by letting anybody know it was Gil's bullet that had taken the sheriff's life. Poe took the cup from his son and finished the coffee, talking around the cup rim: "Maybe one of those detectives spotted who he was."

"Nope." Lank shook his head emphatically. "They ain't got an idea. Neither have all them angry folks. They just want to find and string up ever' last manjack of us. Talk was they did pick up a couple of the boys yesterday as they was crossing the pass out of the county. Santos and Jake. Drilled 'em both dead, the barkeep said. He never said they tried to give up, but I reckon the posse never said neither. Talk was McKelvey had to put a guard on our boys to move 'em over to Repville for trial. It's got that bad."

"Meantime," Dundie muttered, "old Boiler Britches stays on and bides his time. Damn him. He'll not be satisfied till he's cleaned out the last of us."

Nearly half the gang had escaped, but most of them had lost any taste for staying in Leedstock County. Things had been going almost unbelievably smoothly until suddenly McKelvey's meat-grinder of a trap had snapped on them. Most of those who showed up at the caves had come only to demand their share of past loot. Dundie had told them to get it if they dared; somebody who was captured was bound to tip off the law about the location of the gold, and even if they reached it ahead of the law, how would they transport the heavy metal away in a hurry? The original plan had been to convey it down to Mexico by muleback across secret trails by night, in easy stages. They had waited too long and pushed their luck too far, and now they'd have to write off the gold, that was all. Except for the few who decided to stick by—Dandy Mack, Poe and Gil Lockhart, Pima Jack and the two Barrows brothers—they had cursed Dundie to a man and had ridden away.

Poe cared little one way or the other. Since he and Gil had nowhere else to go, they were as well off with Dundie as any place. Eventually Dundie would return to Mexico; when he did, they might find a place of sorts with him and even a chance for a halfway normal life. Poe still hoped that time and a steady hand would curb Gil's wildness. Even so, he felt a glum sense of personal defeat; no matter where they went or how they accommodated themselves to whatever the future might hold, they would live out their lives as fugitives from their home country.

At first he'd found a faint encouragement in realizing that Wye, the only witness to Landrum's killing, had apparently told nobody after all. But all that meant was that Wye was having a hell of a tussle within himself, and Gil's life was too important to stake on a brother's whim of conscience.

Their decision to stay with him had pleased Dundie, who had been cryptically talking of one last, large job to be done before they left for Mexico. It would be something different, simple to pull off, yet so big that every man's share of it would be a lion's share—those who stuck with him would be rich. For now they would have to be satisfied with that, because he was taking no chances on another betrayal; they would be told everything when the time was ripe to move.

Dandy Mack McMurdo was chewing on a cold biscuit. He swore abruptly and spat it out, and came to his feet. "The hell with all this! I'm tired of cold grub and freezing my ass off every night because we can't build a goddamn fire! Christ, a man can't even take a shot at game or stir out of this place without worrying about a posse climbing on his back. I had enough!"

"Simmer down," Dundie told him coldly. "You said you wanted in on this last job. All right, you've waited this long. You can stand another day or so."

"The hell with you," Dandy Mack said with a savage arrogance. "I don't know one damned thing about this job of yours. What I do know is it's a short ride to the border and across. And I know where it's warm the year around and living is so easy a few pesos will insure a life of modest

89

splendor." His eyes swept about him. "Anybody with me?"

Ed Barrows lay wrapped in his blankets just inside the cave. He husked, "Lank talks for us both."

"Why, Ed'll be on his feet in 'most no time." Lank waggled his head gently. "Seems wise we line out south from here right away. All these wild-eyed posses around full of hanging fever, these mountains is no place for a man with colored blood, even happen he was honest."

"All right," Dundie said icily. "There's a fortune almost for the taking, but if any of you tender spring peaches can't withstand a touch of hardship and a minor risk or two to get your fingers on it, ride out now."

Dandy Mack's eyes were cool and yellowed in the bad light; he said, "I might be more inclined to wait if I had some idea of the job. We've stuck by you, Clem, though we haven't a cent to show for it. I won't buy another pig in the poke—if I'm in, I want to hear what the deal is now, all of it."

Dundie dropped his chin in thought; finally he nodded. "Ye'll hear what I know," he said. "But mark you this—not one of ye who hears me out now will ride out of the camp afterward. Not till the job's over and done and we split to go our ways. Do ye ken me?"

Quietly Lank Barrows laid his plate aside and rose slowly, stiffly, to his feet. "Then I reckon we best be on our way, Ed and me. More I done thought on it, more uneasy I gets in my bones. So far we been lucky an' the living been easy. But your luck is changed, Clem. Seems like ever'thing went wrong all at once. Robbery done fell through, gang got busted up, Ed got shot, all that gold we done stole lost, an' now laying low with all them white man posses a-looking for us. I'm thinking you got what our ol' black granny call a *juju* on you, Clem—ain't nothing going to break right for you from here on. Smart man'll do to ride away whilst he's able."

Surprisingly Dundie smiled. "Superstitious mishmash, but I like plain speaking. I ken ye, Lank, and no hard feelings. Anyway three or four men will be all that's needed for this job. But ye needn't ride out yet; wait'll Ed's on his feet again. For now, I'll thank the two of ye to step out in the trees while I talk to the others."

Lank helped Ed labor to his feet and held him upright as
90

they moved off away from the cave to a little grove of scrub pine. Dundie said, "Anybody else?" He flicked his stare across each of them in turn. "Now, the whole of it is—we're going to kidnap Barrett Fancher's wee grandson and ransom him back for two hundred thousand dollars."

There was a moment of dead silence, broken softly by Dandy Mack: "Just like that."

"Just like that. The little fellow is the apple of his grand-daddy's eye; the old man would part with his whole fortune to see him safely returned. We'll ask for a fifth of a million dollars—not a cent more or less. That much Fancher can comfortably scrape up in a short time—and that's important. We'll want to conclude the transaction as quickly as possible and clear out fast."

"We'll need to move a hell of a lot faster than that," Dandy Mack said cuttingly. He sounded worried and angry; he was committed and he didn't like it now. "That old bastard will turn hell inside out to run us down if—"

"He will, and no if," Dundie snapped. "But not while we have the boy. Our necks will be the safest in the county until the boy's back in Fancher's hands."

"The little boy," Smoky said slowly. "You will see he is not hurt? That he is go back safe?"

"Speaking for my part, lass, ye can depend on it. And old Fancher himself'll never make a move that would endanger the lad. Gil, ye know your grandfather. Is that a good bet or no?"

Gil chewed and swallowed a hunk of biscuit. "Sounds right to me. Only I think we ought to take the old man for a real piece of cash while we're about it. He can get a sight more than two hundred thousand together in a hurry if he has to."

"No, no; we'll not be greedy. The laddie who goes too far is in a fair way to tripping himself up."

Poe gave his son a brief, narrow-eyed glance. In the last few days he had noticed a hard substrata he hadn't suspected, cropping up more and more in Gil's manner. He'd told himself it was only the shift in their condition. There had been easy living in Jenny Camp; a man hunted and hungry had an excuse for showing a surly and callous streak. But maybe it was more. If Gil had no reason to love Barrett Fancher, he might give at least a passing thought to the fact that little Benny Yarbrough was his half-brother—a small and frail boy in no condition to be exposed to the hardship of being kidnaped, as Gil was well aware. If sometimes against instinct and better judgment a man did a thing he was not proud of, he could still have the grace to be troubled by his action because this was part of being a thinking and feeling man. Poe could excuse Gil for getting ugly; this indifference to even a twinge of regret was another thing.

Poe decided it was time for him to speak up. "Clem," he said flatly, "there's still a risk. From what Ben said in his letters to me, the boy's health is bad. You bring him up here, if this kind of weather holds, he could take really sick."

"I agree. It's why we'll kidnap his lady nurse along with the boy. She'll see the lad's kept dry and warm, and attend to his wants. A cave will shelter the both of 'em, and one man can stand guard at its mouth." He eyed Poe narrowly. "You still don't like it."

"Not any part of it, but I done plenty things I didn't like before now. What I'm wondering is how you're going to take the woman and kid off Yarbrough's ranch without raising the roof. Plenty of risk right there."

"I will," Dundie said softly. "Rather, we all will. I think you've all heard enough. And you're all in it now. No man of you had better try backing down." Dundie's tone had hardened. He considered any resistance a test of his authority; in salvaging his ego he'd tolerate no more of it. He waited in a kind of deadly silence for Poe to say more, and when he didn't, went on more easily, "You'll hear the rest of the details when we're ready to move, not before. Once the ransom's paid over, we'll push down to Mexico in a hurry."

Dandy Mack said sullenly, "We still need food."

"Never ye worry; I'll see to that matter all right." Dundie's tone was curt and cryptic; he considered the discussion closed, and nobody objected.

Smoky now gathered up the few dishes, saying, "I will wash these." She walked away into the trees. Poe yawned, then stood up and idled across the clearing; he built a smoke as he stretched the cramps out of his legs.

There was a bleak worry in him. Voicing any more objections to Dundie's plan would put him on dangerous ground. In fact there had been an element of danger in his rejoining Dundie after the train fiasco, for as the newest member of the gang, he'd be the one most open to suspicion. But he'd correctly reasoned that Dundie and the others, like Gil, would fix the blame on the mysterious inside man whose identity only Dundie knew.

Yet in the last couple of days, Poe had sensed a new hostility on Dundie's part, though the feeling was nothing he could pin down. It had begun just after Dundie's return from a long ride he had taken for the purpose, Poe had guessed, of meeting and confronting his inside helper. Whatever the fellow had told him had been enough to change Dundie's opinion about the manner of his betrayal. Dundie still had his doubts of course, doubts to which Poe was sure he owed his life. Dundie was a careful man; he could also be absolutely ruthless if he thought the situation demanded it. The least wrong move by Poe would be his last.

Yet everything in his nature bucked against this kidnaping. No matter how carefully it was planned, there was risk to a small boy and a woman. He had the odd, fleeting thought that McKelvey had been right; he had really changed, and before he'd realized it was happening, Benny Yarbrough and his nurse had begun to share the aura of his concern that only Gil had occupied until now.

Poe took the cigarette from his lips, his fist crumpling it unlit. If only there were some way to get word to McKelvey. Out beyond these few trees was a stretch of barren, broken country where, if he made a break, he'd be hunted down in short order. He would stand a better chance on horseback, but he would have to reach the canyon where the horses were roped in. In doing so, he'd expose himself to Pima Jack, who could easily pick him off from his high vantage point. The eagle-eyed half-breed was not only a dead shot, he had a fanatical loyalty to Dundie. Nor could Poe desert the gang while there was Gil to think about: that was his real dilemma.

The only thing he could do for Benny and his nurse, Poe bleakly realized, was to stick by Dundie and be ready to help them in any way that he could.

As he walked slowly, Poe became aware of the nearby stream that chuckled across this plateau out of the high

93

country; its tinkling rush was an intrusion on his thoughts. Now he saw Smoky kneeling on the bank, scrubbing each dish clean with her hand and then laying it on the grass. She grinned briefly up at Poe as he halted beside her. "You men," she chided. "You no have better to do, maybe you catch fish here."

"That's a thought." Poe dug out his makings again and started to roll another cigarette. His hands paused then as his gaze touched for the first time a large purpling bruise on Smoky's brown skin at the base of her neck. Her loose-necked blouse had slipped a little sideways when she knelt, exposing the welt.

She noticed his look; she rubbed a wet hand gently over her neck and said flatly, "Yes. You wonder, and is so. Gil does this."

Poe felt just faintly numb. "And before this?"

"Sometime. Not so much before now. It is this bad life up here, hiding an' worry, I think. Is not so bad for a man when he has somethin' he can make hurt, an' I do not mind so much if is easier for him this way. But was not so bad before. Do not say I tell you, eh?"

Not so bad before Gil's nerves had been rubbed raw by killing a man was what she unwittingly meant, Poe grimly knew—yet he didn't doubt she had been taking this same heavy-handed abuse all along. Poe felt a quiet sickness. Even by his old standards, there were some things a man never did, and if he'd ever given the matter any thought, he would have called a woman-beater the lowest thing there was. It was a breed all but unknown among Westerners, whether they were honest men or outlaws. And now, Poe thought with a kind of helpless misery, *Gil—Gil, why?*

No real question, because he already knew the answer: there was a streak of the same secretive viciousness in Gil's nature that you saw in the kid who tore off the wings of flies and pushed little kids into the mud for pure pleasure. Until now Poe had caught only moody hints of the cruelty Gil had been taking out on Smoky. And in a way there was no understanding it. Gil was far from a coward; this dirty-nosed meanness belonged to a part of him that hid like a thief under the open face of a bawdy and reckless boy.

And in the end none of this really mattered because he was your son, the only immortality a man could be sure of,

94

and worthy of all your blind and loyal fury to shelter and save him.

Smoky had finished with the dishes. She sat cross-legged and watched her hand as she idly swished it through the water. "I have dream sometime. I would like get Gil away from this and make home an' have his children. Maybe in Mexico this could be, eh? So much I want this, but is dream only."

Poe said quietly, "You hang onto that dream, kid. We'll see."

For he knew one thing with a sudden and savage determination: that he was going to straighten Gil up if he had to kick hell out of him. There would be time for that after he got him out of this jackpot with Dundie. That came first, and God help McKelvey or Dundie or anyone else who got in his way.

CHAPTER FOURTEEN

Wye Lockhart sat on a bench with his back against the brick wall, watching Tacey clean out her father's desk. The sheriff's office and the street outside were quiet; there were no sounds but Tacey's small movements as she emptied the drawers, one by one, of the useless and not-quite-discarded trivia of half a man's lifetime.

She'd been pale but calm till now, as she came across the stubby, blackened briar, one Wye had often seen clamped unlighted in Clete Landrum's teeth at moments of quiet talk or reflection at day's end. A little sob caught in her throat, and Wye came to his feet and went over to the desk.

"Tace, let me do this."

"No. I have to. I'll be through in a minute." She tucked the pipe into a portmanteau open on the desk, and pulled out another drawer.

Wye said disapprovingly, "You should throw all this stuff away."

Tacey looked at him with her eyes mirroring a faint

95

shock, and he instantly wished he hadn't spoken. "I will," she said then, softly. "But not yet, Wye. You—you can't just let go of somebody you loved all at once. The pain would be too much. These things are all that remain of Dad except the memories—isn't it little enough? After Mother died, Dad and I had nobody but each other—and now I have no—"

"Yes," Wye said urgently. He took her hands. "Tacey, you have. Don't you know that?"

"Yes . . . yes, I suppose I do. Part of my mind knows, anyhow." She smiled, a little wanly. "I'm afraid you'll have to wait for the rest to catch up with it."

Wye said, "I'm a patient man," and managed a smile before dropping her hands and walking restlessly to the front window. An oblong of barred sunlight fell through it, steep-slanting with early afternoon.

"Wye."

Her gentle voice brought him around, and he saw the open concern in her face. "I've been so full of myself," she murmured, "that I suppose you'd thought I hadn't noticed. But I have, Wye. At first I thought it was just . . . all that's happened. But it's more, isn't it?"

"Why, what do you mean, Tace?" The falseness of his counter was so transparent to Wye himself that he felt a slow flush crawl out of his collar.

Tacey sighed. "I don't know. That's just it. And I guess I won't till you're ready to tell."

"Nothing to tell." Wye's tone was matter-of-fact again, nearly pleasant; his mask was firmly in place for the moment.

Tacey nodded almost imperceptibly, then went quickly through the last drawer. She dropped a handful of items into the portmanteau and shut it, and took her leave with the barest murmur of goodbye. As the door closed behind her, Wye swung restlessly back to the window. The stiffness drained from his face, leaving only a haggard misery as he watched her go down the street. *If I tell her,* he thought, *she'll likely hate me. Not just because he's my brother, but because I covered up for him this long.*

For he could find little that was noble even on the surface of his not revealing that it was Gil who'd killed Clete Landrum. He was honestly sickened by the knowledge—

96

God, yes—almost as sickened as he was by his own silence. But he could have turned a killer brother in, or so he thought, if that were all there was to it. What really held him mute was the simple fear of losing Tacey. And even that was dwindling next to the deeper, numbing fear that all his preciously held values were as flimsy as eggshells. The real test of a man was how hard he could bear down when the heel of justice was on his own neck—and by that test he'd failed miserably.

Now he came alert, watching down the street as four riders came into Leedstock on the north road. They pulled up by the livery stable and dismounted, and Wye saw they were McKelvey and the three detectives who'd stayed on with him in Leedstock. McKelvey passed his reins to one of his companions, then came this way across the street, stiff-jointed with exhaustion, his suit dusty. He spoke to Tacey and tipped his hat, passing her.

At McKelvey's knock, Wye told him to come in. McKelvey gave him a nod that lacked its usual curtness, and moved slowly over to the desk and slacked with a vast sigh into the swivel chair. These past days of organizing posses, riding out dawn till dusk, keeping up an unrelenting search for Clem Dundie and his remaining henchmen, had worn Barton McKelvey to a fine shadow. The keen lines of his face were blurred by a gray stubble; he looked every month of his sixty-six years, and then some.

He rasped a hand over his unshaven chin and said, "Christ," and was unspeaking for ten seconds then. "Don't know why I dropped in. Seems a waste of good words to keep telling you I've turned up nothing."

"You can always give it up." An ill humor shaded Wye's tone. "How do you know Dundie's still out there in those mountains?"

"He is. Hell, a feeling is all. I can't tell you why; I just know."

"Well, suppose he is? You were hired to stop the raids, and they're stopped. If he's still in the country, he's in no position to start up again."

"No," McKelvey said mildly. "But I'll get him or else learn for sure that I've run him clear back to Mexico. Otherwise it's a job half-finished. Might call this a kind of eleventh commandment with me."

"Gospel according to St. Bart."

McKelvey didn't reply for a moment, only eyed him in a speculative and unruffled way. "That could be," he conceded. "What kind of a burr's up your tail, if I may ask? I've been wondering."

"Nothing. What makes you say there is?"

"Listen, boy." McKelvey let his weight creak the chair forward and he set his palms on his knees. "There's men who just naturally wear their consciences like a badge, all clean and shining. That's just fine till it picks up a little smudge; then it makes 'em fit to tie. Take you—lately you've been grouchy as a bear with a sore foot and making yourself pretty damn silly by insisting you're not."

"That's my business."

"It always is, but the people who have to deal with you have to take your guff too, and that's their business." McKelvey settled back in the chair and stiffly raised one boot to the desk's edge, crossing the other carefully over it. "Ahhh . . . better. One more thing, sonny, and then I'll shut up. Whatever's been gnawing at you has been gnawing deeper every day—that's clear as spring water. You're kind of young in your feelings, but you're smart enough in the head—enough to know you can't hold it in forever. You can let it out or go plumb crazy. That's the choice. If I was you, though, I wouldn't be much longer deciding."

Wye pivoted around, anger burning in him. Before he could let the words out, the office door was flung open. Benjy, his grandfather's valet, stood there, out of breath. "Mister Wye—you have to come—"

"What is it?"

"Ran all the way to tell you . . . your little brother—Benny—kidnapped—"

McKelvey's boots thumped on the floor; he brushed roughly past Wye and crossed to the colored youth, seizing him by the shoulder. "Where? How? By who?"

Benjy shook his head. "All I'm to tell you is hurry to Mr. Fancher's office, sir . . . both of you."

McKelvey was out the door on the instant, and Wye followed him. The two of them claimed their horses at the livery and rode out fast on the river road toward Fancher's Mining and Milling Company.

In less than fifteen minutes, they stood in Barrett

98

Fancher's lavish office listening to Ben Yarbrough tell what he knew of the kidnaping. Yarbrough sat hunched in a deep armchair, head bent; his words held a father's stunned and strangled despair that made a man wince to hear. ". . . . boy's health is poor—his nurse, Miss Chaney, tended to pamper him. Several people suggested that he needed a bit of rough-and-tumble living, and I'd ordered Miss Chaney to give him daily outings, extending the walks a bit farther each day. She's a creature of habit, you see—set a particular time each day, took him out in the same area, and extended each walk an unvarying distance farther than the one before. She'd established a firm pattern, so I imagine it didn't prove difficult, once the plan had been laid, to pick up the two of them quite a safe distance from the house. . . ."

McKelvey broke in crisply, "Anybody at the house hear anything?"

"No. I'd left for town right after the noon meal, and immediately afterward Miss Chaney had taken Benny for his walk. All the hands were on the range, and only the cook and his roustabout were left. They were in the cookshack when a horseman galloped by and heaved a rock with the note through the window."

"Then one of them came after you?"

"Yes. Hank—the roustabout—caught up with me halfway between Talon and town. I rode directly back, hoping against hope there'd been a mistake—or just a vicious prank of some kind. I went over the ground, of course. The signs of a scuffle and the prints of three men were clear, and we followed the tracks a ways—but they'd taken pains to cover ground where you couldn't track a whole herd—"

McKelvey put in, "I should think the woman would have screamed." His manner was cool and alert; he was leaving no point untouched.

Yarbrough shook his head wearily. "It happened too far from the main buildings, and nobody could've gotten to the spot in time to do any good."

McKelvey was holding the crumpled ransom note, and now he carefully smoothed it out on his knee and read it again, this time aloud: " 'We have taken your son and his nurse. They will be well so long as you follow orders explicitly. You are to send a single man as your messenger.

99

He will come to the red monument rock at the mouth of Bleeker's Pass tomorrow night at exactly midnight. He will bring two hundred thousand dollars in paper currency and deposit it by the cairn of rocks he will find heaped at the foot of the monument. If these instructions are obeyed, and there is no attempt at trickery, your son and the woman will be returned safely. If not, the consequences will be on your head—and Barrett Fancher's.'" He glanced up, observing wryly, "At least that leaves no doubt that Dundie's still in the vicinity, as I said."

"Dundie." Barrett Fancher was still facing the window with his hands knotted behind his back. He had been standing that way when they had entered the room, and had barely looked around. Nor did he now, but his voice was rock-steady. "How do you know it's Dundie?"

"A man of considerably more than ordinary education wrote this. Dundie was training at the University of Edinburgh before he was chased out of Scotland." McKelvey reached out to lay the note on the desk between himself, Fancher and Yarbrough, as if presenting it for arbitration.

"My God—" Yarbrough's voice, already vibrant with tension, cracked at last; he buried his face in his hands. "He's so little—so weak—"

Barrett Fancher turned slowly now, hands still behind his back, and Wye felt a thin shock. A stranger might have failed to notice what was instantly obvious to Wye: for the first time in his memory, all the briskness had run out of his grandfather, like grain out of a split jutesack. The flesh of his bony face had a dull and colorless texture like faded cloth—it may have been partly the gray daylight—and somehow he seemed suddenly old, unbelievably old.

"Easy, Ben. And put the real fault where it belongs, why don't you?" He added to McKelvey and Wye, "The blame is mine, really. Ben was sparing me when he said that 'several people' had advised exercise for the little fellow. It was directly after I'd made a direct suggestion that Ben gave Miss Chaney the orders for those daily outings."

"A little late to be setting blame." McKelvey gestured at the note. "The thing is, what do you want to do?"

"I'd hoped you might advise me. Pay them, of course, if it will guarantee Benny's safety. But will it?"

McKelvey ran a finger along his white mustache, deliberating. "I'd guess he'd be safe in any case—Miss Chaney too—whether you paid or not. I couldn't answer for all of his men, but I know Dundie well enough. He'd bluff, certainly, to get what he wants, but harming a woman or a little boy isn't his way. The only danger as I see it is that whether you pay or not, he might keep the boy and woman with him awhile to ensure his own safety."

Fancher nodded as he sank slowly into his desk chair, gripping the arms. "There's sense to that. I'd hunt him to hell, by God, once I was sure Benny was safe."

"He knows it." McKelvey paused a long, dry moment. "There's also the possibility that the two hundred thousand is to be merely a down payment—that he means to hold onto the boy and bleed you for all he can."

"Think he will?"

Again McKelvey thought a moment, then shook his head. "No. My guess, he'll head for Mexico directly he has his hands on the money. Two hundred thousand is a reasonable amount to expect a man of your means to scrape together in a few hours. He's a hunted man, don't forget; even with the boy as a hostage, his hide's in danger as long as he stays in these mountains. And don't forget that reward you put on his head—it's caused quite a few people to put aside their work and join the hunt. If any of them should stumble on Dundie's hangout, they'd take some long chances to try for that head money."

For the first time, Fancher's composure was visibly broken; he jerked as if stung. "I didn't think of that," he said very quietly. "My God."

"As I see it," McKelvey went on matter-of-factly, "that's the only real danger to the boy, aside from his poor health. All you can do about it is send out men to every ranch and farm in the basin. I'd reckon they'll all comply with a request to call off the hunt, seeing a boy's life is at stake. You can pay the ransom per instructions." He leaned forward, tapping his finger lightly on the desk. "As to whether Dundie'll let the boy and woman go as soon as he has the money, I'd say the chances are fifty-fifty. That he'll balance the value of a pair of prime hostages for his own safety against the likelihood of the boy taking dangerously

101

ill—and what the extra burden of a couple captives will mean to his speed in getting to the border and across as quickly as possible."

"In any case, I'll get the money together immediately," Fancher said with a naked sincerity. "All I care about is seeing Benny returned to us safe and sound." He laced his hands together on the desk and fixed a bleak stare on his thumbs. "Who'll take the money to the designated place?"

Ben Yarbrough raised a haggard face. "I will, sir. They may be willing to return Benny at once, and if so—"

"They won't," McKelvey interrupted calmly. "They'll wait a spell after the money's left before moving in to pick it up—to assure themselves there's no trap. You'll never catch a sight of them. Anyway, Mr. Yarbrough, you're understandably upset—both of you gentlemen are too involved in the matter to handle it with calm heads. And for the boy's sake, the man who's sent with the money should be cool-headed as well as trustworthy."

Fancher nodded crisply. "You're right, as usual. At the same time, though, we mustn't let word of the kidnaping or the ransom get beyond this room—I've already cautioned Benjy to keep still. In the first place, there are damned few men I'd trust with two hundred thousand dollars. In the second, a lone messenger would be a tempting target for anybody who took a fancy to the money—meaning every tough nut in Leedstock County. That leaves you or Wye, then."

"Wrong," McKelvey said dryly. "It leaves Wye. If Dundie and his boys should be waiting for the messenger and see he's me, they'd think it was a trap. Mr. Lockhart, on the other hand, is the little fellow's half-brother; he'd have a legitimate concern for his safety. I needn't point out that whatever happens, he'll neither lose his head nor attempt rash heroics."

"Good," Barrett Fancher said unhesitatingly. "I was thinking the same thing. Willing, boy?"

"Yes. Of course." A warm complex of feelings swept Wye. He had always felt a nagging doubt of the measure of his grandfather's trust, just as he'd felt a silent resentment all these days at McKelvey's apparent lack of confidence in him. Both of these unvoiced angers were suddenly reduced

102

to zero, and he felt about equal parts of embarassment and relief.

"That's settled." Fancher came abruptly to his feet, brisk again. Wye guessed that now a course of action had been decided, his grandfather would keep himself occupied as usual, diverting himself from the ravage of doubts and dreads. "It's not over eight miles to Bleeker's Pass." Fancher said, "so time's no concern—yet. But let's get cracking. Ben, you round up all the paper currency available at the bank and get it back here. I'll scrape up what I have on hand, and send out messages to my creditors. McKelvey, I'd appreciate it if you and Wyatt would give the bank money an armed escort back here."

The three of them—McKelvey and Yarbrough and Wye—left the plant and quickly covered the mile and a half to Leedstock, and entered the frame building that housed the bank. Inside, on a rail-enclosed platform that commanded the room, sat two watchful guards posted to protect the milled gold in the vault, each armed with a rifle and a shotgun. Yarbrough collected all the available currency from the clerks and told them to close down their cages for the day. Then he led the way to his office and told McKelvey and Wye to wait here; the rest of the bank's paper money was in the underground vault. He disappeared into a long, brick-walled corridor that ramped down to the vault.

Alone now with the old detective, Wye felt obliged to voice his awkward thanks. "About what you did—I mean speaking up for me to Gramps—"

"He'd already decided you were the man for this job; all I did was confirm his opinion. Why not? I did you no favor, Mr. Lockhart; a man proves his own worth. Other men see it and treat him accordingly. Why thank either of two old men for simply recognizing ability and integrity?"

Wye could not help flushing with pleasure; he had to lower his eyes. "Funny," he murmured. "I had the idea you might be tired of seeing me feel sorry for myself and were trying to jolt me out of it."

"Now why in hell would I do that?"

Wye lifted his glance, and for the first time thought he saw a twinkle liven the detective's frosty eyes. "All right then," Wye told him, "I won't suggest you did. But if you're

103

finally trusting me, I wish you'd tell me what you refused to before. How in the devil did you get the information about Dundie's train raid that enabled you to lay the trap you did?"

"I'd say you're about ready to hear how," McKelvey said without expression. "Your pa told me."

Wye listened in stunned silence while McKelvey told him all of it—how he had gone to Jenny Camp with the intention of bringing Poe back if he found him there, but how the upshot of the encounter had been his enlisting Poe's help. Not knowing at the time who he could trust, McKelvey had told Fancher, Yarbrough, and Wye himself that he hadn't found Poe with Dundie's gang. Since Dundie had made known his elaborate plans several days in advance in order to carefully coach his men on every detail, Poe had found no difficulty in getting word to McKelvey at their twice-a-week rendezvous.

"But," Wye cut in with a kind of wild impatience now, "what made you think you could trust him? A man of his background and reputation—he could have been putting you on in order to—"

"You self-righteous cub," McKelvey snapped. "Did it ever occur to you to wonder why your pa joined up with Dundie—why he broke prison in the first place?"

After a full quarter-minute, Wye said in an oddly blank voice, "I suppose it might have been—Gil."

"Exactly. It was to have been a trade. Your pa wanted to set Gil on the straight and narrow. I agreed to do all I could for them both in exchange for all I needed to know about Dundie's next move."

"But what about your friend that he . . . didn't he?"

"He didn't deny he was responsible for Rydell's death. He did persuade me it was unintentional. A bad break. Your pa is a changed man, young fellow—I read that much in him, and it's what convinced me to take a chance with him. He proved out, all right. He was to have given himself and your brother up to me, and I can only guess he didn't have the chance. Important thing is, he's proved himself."

Wye came abruptly to his feet, almost knocking over his chair, and strode to the window. He stared out, his jaw set. The force of what McKelvey had said was balling in his belly like an indigestible mass. There was a slow throb

104

starting in the back of his skull; too much of his thinking demanded to be suddenly revised, and he felt overwhelmed, a little stunned.

It was the crowning touch to everything that had happened lately, all of it mingling in his mind with silent shouts of confusion—Clete, Gil, Tacey, his father—as though the world he'd built for himself were crumbling away under his feet and he was swimming in empty space.

The clicking echo of Ben Yarbrough's steps coming back along the corridor to the office jarred Wye back to the reality of now. There was a job to do, and he gripped this thought with a gray reflex of false relief; he would not have to worry about anything else for a time. Not while there was the job to be done.

CHAPTER FIFTEEN

Dundie and Dandy Mack and Gil came riding into camp about sunset, leading their captives. The woman was mounted on a spotted horse Dundie had taken along for the purpose, and she held the boy in front of her. Poe and Smoky had been talking idly by the cave mouth, and now Smoky ran over to Gil as he slipped off his mount. The others dismounted too. Poe went over to them and Dundie gave him a cold grin and handed him the spotted horse's leadrope. He said, "Hold that," and moved to the horse's left side, lifting up his arms. "All right, miss, pass me down the boy."

Margaret Chaney didn't say a word, but she held Benny more tightly to her; there was a cold venom in her gaze. Now Poe saw the darkening bruise on her cheek and the tear in her shirtwaist, and a thin anger touched him.

Dundie snapped his fingers. "Come now, mistress; let's not be difficult. You'll not be here past one night if all goes well, and no need to make things more unpleasant than they already are."

After a long moment, she placed the boy in his hands.

105

Dundie set him on the ground and then helped her down. He pointed at one of the cave mouths pocking the ridge and told her curtly, "Over there. The place has been made as comfortable as possible for you, and ye'll not be molested."

Still wordlessly, she gathered Benny in her arms again and walked to the cave. Poe said softly, "Who manhandled her, Clem?"

Dundie eyed him an unpleasant moment. "She fought us. Took all three of us to hold her, and there was nothing for it."

"Who hit her in the face?"

Dundie frowned. "Don't ask questions for whose answers ye'll have no stomach, Poe. Your son did that. It suits his taste, using a heavy hand on a woman."

"And you stood for it." Poe's tone was whisper-light. "You've sunk a long way, Clem."

A slow flush crawled into Dundie's face. He reached out and took the reins from Poe's hand, saying wrathfully then, "Do I need to remind ye of whose blood runs in his veins? Go look in a mirror if ye need that reminder, damn you!"

Pima Jack had loped silently up and was expectantly eyeing Dundie, who said curtly, "Take these animals to the canyon, Jack. Then saddle up your own and get back here."

Pima Jack picked up the horses' reins and headed into the trees, leading all four animals. Dandy Mack McMurdo coughed gently; he was lighting a cigar as he fixed Poe with his light, mocking gaze. Poe settled a hard stare on him, hoping he would say something, anything that would offer Poe an excuse to slug him. But Dandy Mack chuckled out a cloud of smoke and turned away.

Poe swung his glance toward Gil and Smoky at the far end of the clearing. She was talking quietly, earnestly to Gil; he was sucking on a cigarette and scowling as though he'd like to hit her. Poe flexed his fist, thinking, *Let him try. Let me catch him hitting a woman and he'll be nursing a busted neck.* After a moment, though, the rage drained out of him and only a sadness and bitterness was left. He could no longer deceive himself even momentarily that Gil was just wild in the way of his own young manhood; the last few days had eroded away the last of the cheerful scamp that Gil had seemed to be, and what remained was a bedrock of meanness that took a real pleasure in itself.

Poe bleakly wondered if he might bust such a streak out of his son as he would out of a mean horse. Even if he got the chance, it would be a bitter and thankless chore. In any case, he couldn't do more than hold on and wait for the chance to try.

Just now his concern lay with little Benny Yarbrough and his nurse. There was nothing he could have done to prevent the kidnaping, for he and Smoky had remained in camp when the others had ridden out early today. After Lank and Ed Barrows had pulled out yesterday for Mexico, Dundie had idly observed that they still had more than enough men to handle the job. An extra man would just be in the way, so Poe was left behind—as was Pima Jack, whose position on the ridgetop enabled him to keep an eye out for cruising posses of men who might still be on the hunt for them. Also, obviously, the half-breed had a clean view of the clearing below and would spot Poe at once if he tried to slip away.

Poe could guess why, though Dundie's suspicions of him ran deep by now, he was continuing this cat-and-mouse game. It wasn't in Dundie's cautious nature to keep alive a man for whom he harbored a deep distrust when a word from him would dispose of that man. What held him back was the knowledge that if he and Pima Jack and McMurdo took on one Lockhart, they'd have to take on two, for it would require more than mere suspicion to turn Gil against his father. Dundie was far too careful to like even three-to-two odds, which meant that as long as Poe had Gil's allegiance, he was probably safe.

As for the woman and boy, since they would be safely returned as soon as the ransom was in Dundie's hands, Poe would do neither himself nor them any good by attempting any heroics on their behalf. There was always a chance that something might go awry and they'd need his help, but other than being watchful against that moment, the best he could do was let things ride as they were.

Pima Jack returned to the clearing, leading his horse. Dundie began talking to the half-breed in an underpitched voice, and Poe guessed at the substance of what was said. If Pima Jack started from here now, he would achieve Bleeker's Pass shortly before midnight, when Fancher's messenger should arrive with the money. The half-breed was like a cat in the dark; he would find the pass with un-erring ease. He wouldn't be caught napping for a moment, and if there were any sort of trap afoot, he'd smell it out at once. Most important, perhaps, his loyalty to Clem Dundie was absolute and unquestioning.

After Pima Jack had mounted and jogged away across the plateau, Dundie returned to his cave. During the next couple of hours, though, he was repeatedly at the cave entrance looking out, puffing down one cigar after another to a damp stub.

It was quite late, the smoky web of dusk closing over the high country, when the tattoo of a horse's hoofs on rock brought them all into the clearing, alert. It was still hours to midnight, so this wouldn't be Pima Jack returning from his errand. Everybody looked at Dundie. He drew idly on his cigar with a vast unconcern that made Poe think, *He's expecting somebody for sure.*

Gil muttered something and brought his pistol whispering from leather. Dundie turned his head and said sharply, "Keep it out, but I'll give any order to use it." The rider came past the last trees and into the clearing. Halting his animal, he briefly made a broad and bearlike shape against the fading twilight. He unslung a heavy sack from his pom-mel and stepped down, and now Poe saw that he was Ben Yarbrough.

Ben had changed little. He was heavier and had grown a spade beard, but his broad, boyish, dimpling face was the same, and his boyish plume of sandy hair. He dropped the sack to the ground. "There's the grub you wanted, Clem. Enough to see us a good ways into Mexico." He wore a genial grin. "Surprised, Poe?"

"Some," Poe admitted. "So you're the man on the inside?"

"That's it." Yarbrough had lowered his hand to his side when he let go the sack, and now that hand came back up, brushing his belt. A snub-nosed pistol glinted in his palm, its cocking a crisp, metallic sound in the still air. He leveled it at Poe's belly and said in a careful, wicked voice, "Well, there he is, Clem. The man who sold you out to McKelvey. And this time I'm not guessing."

108

Dundie said very softly, "Ye'd better be *damned* sure, Ben."

"I'm sure," Yarbrough started to say, and then Gil, recovering from his first surprise of seeing his stepfather here, slashed angrily across his words: "What the hell you mean, he sold out? Pa's been with us right along!"

"He has," Yarbrough nodded, "but not for any reason you might have guessed, Gil. I can even tell you how long he's been working for the law and how the scheme between McKelvey and him was set up."

Dundie said impatiently, *"How* d'ye know?"

Yarbrough sparely told them how, when he'd been in the bank vault getting together the available currency as part of the ransom payment, Wye and McKelvey were talking in his office. "They were speaking softly, but not so much I couldn't catch most of what was said." Yarbrough smiled. "Sound carries like the devil down that brick-lined corridor to the vault—almost as if you were standing next to the speaker. Not realizing as much, they spoke distinctly above whispers. Wye asked McKelvey how he'd gotten the information he'd needed about the train raid, and McKelvey said he judged that Wye was ready to hear about that now. He said Wye's pa had told him."

Dundie moved to Poe's side now and lifted the gun from his holster and rammed it in his own belt. His face was hard and intense: "All of it, Ben—all that ye can tell us. How did they first get together?"

For the next five minutes Yarbrough calmly told what he'd heard McKelvey explain to Wye, elaborating here and there to a question by Gil or Dundie or Dandy Mack. It was a thorough and damning explanation, and a gray defeat filled Poe as he listened. There was nothing he could say that would help his case, he knew. Dundie's suspicion had simply been made concrete now, and Dandy Mack was eager to believe the worst of a man who'd twice humiliated him. As for Gil, the brittling shades of change in his voice told Poe all he needed to know. Gil was at first bewildered by Yarbrough's accusation, then hotly denying. But soon he was impressed, and at last, coldly, accepting.

It was Dandy Mack who said with a deep pleasure, "Want me to take him off a ways, Clem?"

Gil said quickly, "Like hell you will!" He looked ready to fight about it, which might have swayed Dundie's answer.

"Forget it, Mack," he said irritably. "Once we've let the woman and boy go, Poe'll be handy to have along till we're over the border. Not as likely a hostage as the two we have now, but better than nothing. Since he's in league with the law, they'll think twice about jumping us while his life's in our hands. Gil, fetch a rope here."

There was a hushed gasp from behind them, yanking Poe's glance around. Margaret Chaney was standing a few yards off in the seeping dusk, a hand pressed to her face. She stared in disbelief at Ben Yarbrough. Their voices must have drawn her from the cave—or likely one voice in particular, Yarbrough's. She'd caught at least some of what had been said. Swiftly turning now, she ran back to the cave.

For a moment it seemed that Yarbrough might go after her, but he didn't. He threw a bulky warbag and his saddle to the ground, asked Dundie where the horses were, and led his mount off to the horse canyon.

"Getting onto dark," Dundie observed genially. "Smoky, build a fire and cook up a bit of that grub, will ye, lass?"

She knelt by the tarp pack that Yarbrough had brought and opened it. Dundie negligently held his gun on Poe until Gil had returned with the piece of rope and secured Poe's hands. Afterward Dundie and McMurdo moved off, leaving the two of them alone for the moment.

As Gil tied his feet, drawing the rope taut with angry yanks, Poe said mildly, "It wouldn't suit you to hear the why, I reckon."

Gil said bitterly, "You got no reason I'd listen to." But a moment later he burst out, "Why *did* you do it, Pa? We could of had the world by the tail, two of us together."

"That's what I wanted," Poe said. "But not this way. That's why I done it, boy. Had to. You wouldn't of listened, just as you won't now. All I'd figured on for now was getting you away from Dundie—"

"And straight into a noose!"

"No. I made the deal with McKelvey pretty much as Ben just told it. But that was before you done for Landrum. That changed everything. I'd meant to stick with Clem as you did, and hope for the best. Maybe a fresh start of sorts down in Mexico. But that don't mean a lot, does it?"

Gil jerked a knot tight and straightened up, saying, "Not a damned thing," before he pivoted on a heel and walked away.

Poe sat on the damp ground hunched against the night's growing chill. He didn't suppose that Gil, no matter how else he felt about his old man, would let anything happen to him, but what was the difference? No matter how things went now, he'd failed. A last slender chance that he might have helped his son was gone, and nothing else meant a damn.

Smoky soon had the fire going; the smell of beans and bacon made a belly-knotting goodness on the cold air. When the others gathered around the blaze to blot up its warmth and eat, Poe was permitted to join them, his hands loosened so he could handle a plate and cup and fork. Smoky loaded a plate and filled a coffee cup, and carried them to the cave where Margaret Chaney and Benny were. She'd already helped the nurse build a small fire by the cave mouth for what cheer and warmth it could give.

Dundie was in good spirits. "I don't mind telling ye, Ben, I was worried for a spell that ye might not get here. Not that your company is indispensable, but we'd have been in a pretty pickle without this food ye brought."

"Well, I had enough of a time getting away," Yarbrough dourly observed. "I had to help old Fancher get the money together, then ride back to Talon and raid the house pantry since it didn't seem safe to buy up a fat grubstake in town— not with that damned hawk-eyed McKelvey around. And then it's a good-five-hour ride to get here, no matter how well a man knows the country."

"Ye made it, all that matters. And from that warbag, it's plain ye mean to quit the basin and come with us. I didn't half believe ye when you claimed you would; it's why I was concerned ye might not even show up tonight."

"How else could I be sure of getting my cut?"

"A point," Dundie said agreeably. "I always did opine that honor among thieves was a pretty fiction. Still ye've built a life for yourself here, a middling fair one founded on honest sweat. Seems a good bit for a man to give up after many years."

"Many years of running to Fancher's beck and call," Yarbrough said softly. "It doesn't set in my belly to be any

111

man's dog—it never did. What's my piece of this job, Clem?"

"Why, a fourth. Fifty thousand dollars. And well worth the price, seeing as it was your idea and you so neatly set things up by having your lad and his nurse take those fine long walks in the mornings."

"Fifty thousand dollars," Yarbrough went on in the same soft way. "Money not worth a damn to me here where I'll never be able to spend it without arousing suspicion. To Mexico with you, later to Argentina—those are my plans. That little empire you made for yourself gave me the idea, Clem—I can build one of my own on the *pampas* where there's even more room for a man to grow, to expand. A small fortune is a big one down there—" he smiled thinly— "And that far apart, no danger we'll ever get in each other's hair."

Dundie chuckled. "I'll own I like the idea. Particularly since there's room for but one gringo overlord in my part of Mexico."

Smoky came back to the fire and filled a plate for herself, remarking, "The *nino,* he is still sleep."

"Are, they comfortable?" Yarbrough asked sharply. "Warm enough?"

"Why don't ye go see for yourself?" Dundie asked in a dry, faintly needling way. "They've plenty of blankets." He set aside his plate and dug out a cigar, remarking, "Ye know, I couldn't say exactly why, but there's something about a man coming out with the idea of kidnaping his own lad that makes my gorge rise. Even, I mean, allowing that he'll be well-treated and safely returned. Not that I'm in any wise excusing the rest of us—kidnaping's a low thing whoever does it. But a man who'll put his own son's kidnap money in his pocket is a special kind of lowlife. Well, it's truly strange how things come out, eh? Who'd have guessed, knowing what they do of your two pasts, that it'd be Poe who finally took the deadrot of respectability in his system, and Ben who'd turn out to have the makings of a truly evil man."

Yarbrough gave him a brief wicked glance, then looked back at the fire. Dundie smoothed the cigar between his lips and lighted it, chuckling once more. "His conscience has been at him, ye'll note; it's why he's silent. That'll pass.

Conscience is a luxury a man can't hold with long and ride this trail. Finally, he'll tell himself that even if his lad will be lacking both mother and father now—though as to that last, he's lost little enough—he'll still have a rich old grandpa. And there it'll end, gentlemen."

CHAPTER SIXTEEN

As the pale drabness of false dawn was flooding the east, Poe stirred sleepily awake to the sound of two riders coming into the clearing. When he groggily raised his head, he saw that one of the horsemen was Pima Jack and that he was holding a gun on the other man.

It took a moment in this pale murk to recognize the second rider—that and the fact that the rider had been sixteen when Poe had last seen him. *It's Wye,* Poe thought, and felt the gray shock go through him as he met his older son's glance for the first time in six years.

Poe was laying by the dead fire in his blankets, half-frozen by the cramping chills of a long high-country night spent on the thinly blanketed ground with hands and feet tightly bound, hardly able to even flex his muscles for warmth.

Gil was on guard duty now, but he'd been lightly dozing on the other side of the fire, rifle across his knees. Now he came awake with a start and got swiftly to his feet, watching his brother in open disbelief. "Wye? What you doing here?"

"Hello, Gil. You'll have to ask somebody else."

Dundie was aroused too, and he came out of his cave and walked to the fire, which was crumbling into a mound of embers. He kicked it up and threw on a few chunks of wood, afterward briskly rubbing his hands above the blaze. Dandy Mack joined them as the half-breed dropped off his horse and held out a thick package to Dundie, who took it and tore open the brown paper wrapping. Kneeling by the fire, he began to methodically count the packets of greenbacks.

Gil looked from Dundie to his brother and again at Dundie, then burst out furiously, "Damn it, Clem, what's he doing here?"

"Who? Oh, the messenger." Dundie didn't look up; he went on counting the money as he talked. "I gave Jack orders to be waiting out of sight by the monument at Bleeker's Pass. All he had to do was step out and take the man who brought the money—" Dundie chuckled— "and bring him to us along with the money. Your saintly father, even allowing he's taken the law's part, doesn't make the likeliest hostage in the world, ye'll admit, Gil. Ye ken that whoever Fancher sent with the money—a man in whom he'd repose a considerable trust—would be far better company to ensure our safety to the border."

"But damn it, Clem—that's Wyatt! He's my brother!"

Dundie looked up in surprise; his light icy stare scanned Wye's face, then Gil's and lastly Poe's. "Well, well," he murmured. "The brother and the son, eh? Never had the honor of meeting your other lad, Poe. Not much resemblance, to be sure, and I'm thinking he's the lucky one."

Poe, being in no position to say anything, didn't reply. Gil said hotly, "Clem, you play hell with my brother's life, I'll make you answer!"

Dundie showed a trace of irritation. "Don't be a fool, boy. Your brother means nothing to me dead. Alive, he's our sure passport to the border—acting sheriff of Leedstock County and a grandson of old Fancher's to boot. So are you, of course, but not a beloved one, I'll wager."

Gil looked sulky; he said nothing.

"Naturally, we'll turn him loose when his usefulness to us is ended. We'd have no reason not to, would we?" Dundie's freckled face relaxed to a boyish grin. "I'll let both your kin go and ask only that ye stick by old Clem. How's that for a bargain?"

Gil nodded, mollified by the charm Dundie could switch on when it suited him. Dundie went on counting the money as Yarbrough joined them. His eyes were bloodshot and blinking; his clothes had a rumpled, slept-in look. He was as surly as a bear with a sore foot, and when Wye said in a soft shocked voice, "Ben! what're you doing here?" Yarbrough didn't bother to glance at him.

114

Dundie thumbed nimbly through the bulk of the money, then tore the wrapping off the last few packets; a folded piece of paper fluttered out. "Hullo, what's this? Well, well. A note from Fancher. He says to return Miss Chaney and the boy promptly and safely, and he'll guarantee our safe conduct out of the country. What would ye think of that, Ben?"

"I know nothing about it."

"That's a lie," Wye said in a baffled, angry way. "You were there when he put the note in with the money. Ben, what *is* this? You're not—" He paused, staring at Yarbrough with comprehension. "So you're the one . . . Ben?"

"Of course he is," Dundie said impatiently, bringing his flat palm down on the paper spread across his thigh. "As to the boy and the lady, Fancher's kept his side of the bargain; I'll keep mine—but I'll take no chances on Fancher's word. Not with that old gray wolf McKelvey still about; no man can be sure what he'll do. So ye'll accompany us to the border, young sheriff. Jack!"

The half-breed glided around his horse, and Dundie held out his hand palm up, tapping each finger for emphasis. "Listen now. Ye'll take the woman and the little boy back to Talon ranch and leave them within sight of the house. Rest of us will break camp at once and strike out south. Will ye have any trouble in overtaking us?"

"No trouble. All white man trail easy follow. Catch up before sun there." He pointed at the deep west.

"All right. Saddle that tame animal the lady rode yesterday; she can hold the boy in front of her. Lively now."

Pima Jack moved off toward the horse canyon at his quick dogtrot. Margaret Chaney had stepped outside the cave and was looking on, and Dundie called to her, "Get the boy ready, Mistress. Ye'll be on your way home in a minute."

Without a word, Yarbrough wheeled and stalked back to his cave, his shoulders hunched. Dundie took the cigar from his mouth, chuckling lightly. "The conscience still. He can't bear to face his lad. It's as well. There'll be a spate of melodramatics if the boy sees him, and that sort of thing before breakfast always did set ill on my belly."

In a few minutes, Pima Jack returned with the saddled

115

horses, and little Benny was awakened. The boy had slept or napped almost continuously since his arrival here, and Poe was surprised when he saw him come from the cave. There was some color in Benny's face; his eyes were bright and lively. When he saw Wye, he yelled and ran over to him. "Hi, Wye! What you doing here? You playing the game too?" Apparently a day and night of this high pure air had been the tonic the boy had needed. As she came up, Margaret Chaney's eyes were sparkling with happiness. It was a strange way for a kidnaping to end, Poe thought: old Fancher would count his two hundred thousand a small loss against the unexpected burst of health in his small grandson and heir.

Dundie assisted Margaret Chaney into the saddle and lifted Benny up in front of her. Pima Jack caught up the leadrope and climbed onto his pinto, and they rode out.

Dundie lost no time now. After a hasty breakfast, the horses were brought from the canyon. They were saddled and packed, the weight of gear and provisons distributed equally among the riders.

A gold-pink sting of true dawn had barely welted the east when they broke camp. They rode single file down the narrow trail Dundie had chosen to carry them off the plateau's south rim and into a gorge that would take them south through a looming arm of peaks.

Dundie had sized up this whole terrain and the best trails many months ago. Just as he'd selected the plateau and the cave hideout with an eye to emergency, so he'd mapped out a route from here to the border through wild and little-known country. Riding in the lead, he held a pace that was steady but not grueling. Next came Smoky, and behind her rode Wye and then Poe, their hands lashed in front of them with pieces of rawhide riata. The others—Yarbrough and Gil and Dandy Mack—brought up a kind of rear guard.

By mid-morning they were deep in the gorge; they nooned between its towering walls, the high sun beating down with a molten fury. Dundie permitted Poe's and Wye's hands to be freed so they could shed their coats, but ordered them bound once more. He was nervous and wary again; he was eager to be across the border. The party hugged what little shade was available under the beetling

116

rims. In a kind of weary, sweat-drenched lethargy, they ate the cold cooked grub that Smoky passed out.

Ben Yarbrough sat a couple of yards away from Poe, looking as if he were eating sawdust. Finally he stared at Poe and said softly, as if he needed to dredge this one thin triumph out of the situation, "I want you to know it was me who got you sent to Coldrock. I tipped off McKelvey that you'd be at my place that night, and we arranged things so that Emmaline and the boys wouldn't find out. Now I want you to know—I want you to think about it."

Poe didn't even look at him or break the rhythm of his chewing. He said unconcernedly, "You're too late, Ben. It don't matter any more. I don't even care why you did it."

"You bastard!" Yarbrough shouted. "I'll tell you why!" He pitched the sandwich and cup he was holding away and came to his feet, his meaty hands fisted. Circles of sweat darkened the underarms of his shirt. "It was Emmaline, damn you! I always hated you for that—I never stopped hating you all those years you had Emmaline—"

"Too bad." Poe set his sandwich down so he could lift his cup between his tied hands. "You pretty well threw me off the other night. Besides you'd had no reason for keeping me informed about the boys all those years I was in Coldrock."

Dundie grimaced. "No reason but a bad conscience," he observed. "Didn't that occur to you, Poe?"

"It did, some." Poe took a swig of tepid water from the cup. "Only I remembered what a snow-white character Ben always had, and so I figured, well—"

"You son of a bitch!" There was a sheen of cold hate on Yarbrough's eyes. He lashed out with a savage kick, his boot glancing off Poe's cheekbone and tearing flesh. The force of it knocked Poe over backward. He rolled onto his side half-stunned, and then lunged to his feet.

"That's enough!" Dundie had gotten up too, and so had Gil, his gun drawn.

Poe raised his bound hands to his bleeding cheek, then held them out. "Not by half, Clem," he said. "Not if you cut me loose for just five minutes."

At another time Dundie might have fancied the idea, but he was worried and harried now; he crackled, "I'm in no damned mood for games!"

117

Yarbrough had dropped warily back a few steps, his ruddy and distorted face glistening with sweat, ready for anything. Dundie pointed a finger at him, saying softly, "Don't try my patience again. Just one more wrong move by you, and you're dead. Understand?"

In saddle again, they rode steadily through the day and left the gorge by late afternoon. As he'd said he would, Pima Jack overtook them shortly thereafter. He reported to Dundie that he had returned Margaret Chaney and Benny Yarbrough to the Talon headquarters without a hitch, leaving them a short distance from the house.

The half-breed took the lead now, guiding the party across the final leg of the mountains by little-known trails he could probably have followed blindfolded. But they were a long way from out of the peaks by sunset when, though hours of daylight remained, a sheer and heat-drained exhaustion forced them to make early camp.

They stopped in a grove of scrubby pine in a wide bowl of valley with good water and grass. Smoky set to cooking supper over a small blaze. While the others hung by the fire, Poe and Wye were isolated with their blankets at one side of the little clearing where they'd be easy to watch.

Not till now had Poe and his older son been thrown together in this sort of semi-privacy, and now that they were, Poe felt an embarrassment. This was a natural chance for them to talk, but what could they have to say to each other? True, Wye hadn't so far displayed any of the bitter or hateful rancor for which Poe had braced himself, but then Wye had always been his mother's son in that respect—as in most every other. Neither of them had ever willingly given Poe a glimpse into his or her private thoughts, so that he'd always been left to guess.

It was Wye who first broke the silence of years, saying in a moderate voice, "I never knew about Ben—giving you away to the law as he did. Somehow that was a bigger shock than his arranging for Benny to be kidnaped."

"He had a good reason, I reckon," Poe said meagerly. "By his own lights, the best of reasons. Your mother."

"I supppose so. I'd never thought a lot about—why people do what they do. I guess it was McKelvey who started me thinking. He meant to, I know now; that's why he'd been almost nothing but harsh with me these weeks

118

we've been working together. He took a special interest in me—I suppose because he'd never had a son—and he saw clearly how twisted up some of my notions were."

"A good pa would have seen that never happened," Poe said quietly. "McKelvey would have been the best."

"The best of *friends*. I already have a father." Poe looked at him and Wye smiled a little and nodded. "He made me see that, too. You find the bad with the good, the good with the bad—if you take somebody at all, you take him in a lump that's never black or white."

"That can be a big lump to swallow."

"It can. I don't think I got it all the way down until today. I was confused as hell." Wye knit his brows. "Everything I'd made of myself, everything I'd thought I wanted, was built around setting myself against whatever I'd believed you stood for. I knew it, and I was damned proud of it. Then—after McKelvey told me why you'd broken out of prison, why you'd gone in with Dundie and what you'd done for us, all for Gil's sake—it all fell apart."

"I reckon finding Ben on the other side mixed things up too."

"No." Wye shook his head thoughtfully. "Never really thought about it before, but Gil was right. In all the years he was our stepfather, though we were treated well enough, there was no real closeness. If Ben had really moved into your place and become any sort of force in our lives, I think we'd both have turned out differently than we did. Good or bad, I don't know—but different. I couldn't have been more surprised to see Ben with Dundie, but that was all." Wye paused. "What really got me was the notion that if I'd been mistaken about you, then everything I'd built around that wrong-headed assumption was just as wrong."

Poe shook his head. "No. All I can see that's wrong—"

"Is my notion. I know. I had to realize that too—that a wrong reason for believing something doesn't make the belief itself wrong." Wye paused now, turning his head till his eyes rested on Gil. His fine jaw hardened under a blur of beard stubble that was darker than his light brown hair. "I'm still a lawman with a sworn duty. I'd lost sight of myself for awhile, and then I wasn't sure any more. Now I am. The law is a part of my life, part of what I've made myself into, and from here on I'll stand by it."

Poe felt a chill dismay as he understood his son's meaning. and yet mingled in was an unexpected wave of pride and affection for Wye that made his eyes sting. He bent his face to keep it in shadow as he said, "I had the idea you hadn't told anybody about who shot Landrum."

Wye gave him a sharp glance. "So he told you?"

"Me, nobody else. One of Dundie's boys was in Leedstock a few days back. The town was buzzing about Landrum's killing, but they didn't know who of us done it."

"They don't know yet," Wye said slowly, "but they will. I don't know if I can make you understand why—but I can't keep it quiet any more. For a while I didn't know any longer what was right or wrong. And there was a girl . . . she's Clete Landrum's daughter. I—well, I want to marry her. And I was afraid if she knew it was my brother who killed her dad, I'd lose her."

Poe gave a dour nod. "And now you ain't afraid, is that it?"

Wye's lips curled around a wry grin. "Just scared as the devil, that's all. Without her, I don't know what I'll—but it doesn't matter. Or rather I can't *let* it matter. I know what I believe in now, and I'm going to live up to it if it kills me."

"Or if it kills your brother, eh?"

Wye leaned toward him. "Look," he said with a hushed, earnest passion, "I didn't expect you to understand. I don't think anybody can unless they're a part of it . . . part of the law. It's the sort of thing that a man who's involved in it comes to put ahead of everything else in his life—everything."

"Including his own kin?"

"Yes—even that. Because I think that a man has to rise above his personal passions into something—something bigger than himself, a thing that's been forged for the good of all men, not what benefits just a few. Pa, I know you'd kick over any set of traces for Gil's sake—or for mine. But we only add up to three people. I don't blame or judge you for feeling as you do, but I can't be that way. If I could make you see—"

"I follow you all right. I ain't lettered, but that don't make a man a jughead." Poe's tone softened. "A man does what he has to, boy. I understand that, all right. Let it go. No

120

need for a set-to over something that won't be coming to a head between us anyhow."

"We can always hope not," Wye said in the same stubborn, murmurous undertone. "But I'm a law officer, and these are holdup men and kidnapers. Gil is an accomplice to robbing and kidnaping, and he's killed a man. My job's to take in any or all of them, and I'll grab at any chance I get—any chance at all."

"You must be sure as Almighty God of yourself."

"No. But I *think* I'm right—and a man can only stand on what he believes is the right course. And pa, you're no different."

Poe was silent then. He did some pondering, but he couldn't find a reply for his son that had a convincing ring even to his own mind. He could only hope that he wouldn't by some blind chance be placed in the intolerable position of having to choose between his two sons.

Smoky had the food bubbling over the fire, and with this tended to, she came over to the prisoners, carrying a canteen and a tin cup. "You like water?"

"Yes, please," Wye said. "Pa?"

Poe nodded, and Smoky filled the cup and handed it to him. Awkwardly holding the cup between his bound hands, Poe drank and then passed the empty cup to Wye. He held it up while Smoky poured it full; his palm skated on the damp metal and the cup slipped, spilling. "Sorry." Smoky filled it again, and Wye drained the cup and said, *"Mil gracias,"* as he handed it back.

Smoky nodded, eyeing both of them with a brooding compassion. "Is too bad for you, all of you Lockhart. Gil and papa and brother, all fight each other, eh?"

"Looks that way," Poe said.

CHAPTER SEVENTEEN

Shortly after they had cleaned up the last of the beans, biscuits, and strong coffee, the whole party except for Gil, who was standing first watch, had rolled wearily into their

121

soogans around the fire. And not very long after that, only Wye was awake, wrapped to his eyebrows in his blanket and feigning sleep.

He lay with his back to Gil and his hands up by his face, hidden by the blanket folds as he patiently tugged with his teeth at the rawhide cords on his wrists. The thorough wetting he'd managed to give them earlier by spilling the cup of water on his wrists had turned the stiff raw leather slick and malleable, and he had worked at straining and stetching it to greater length when nobody was looking.

Now, with the dampness of spittle and the steady pull of his aching jaws, he slowly stretched the rawhide a few fractions of an inch farther. Exerting a strong and controlled effort, Wye began to slip his right hand slowly free of the tortured loops. He put out all his strength and felt skin tear along his knuckles—then he was free.

He groaned and stirred as if tossing in his sleep; he heaved over on his other side so that he was now facing the fire and could watch Gil sitting just beyond it. Wye kept the blanket high around his chin, his hands covered, eyes slitted nearly shut as he studied his brother. Gil gave him one disinterested glance, then looked back at the fire. It was foolish of him: a man who stared at fire would be momentarily blinded when he looked away from it. But then none of them were expecting trouble from the prisoners— why should they? It would be only good sense for Poe and Wye to stay docile and stay alive, and go free when the border was behind them.

Under the blanket now, Wye pulled the loose cords off his left wrist and stuffed them in his pocket, and slowly and roughly massaged feeling back into his stiff hands. Against the cold urgency he felt, he forced his thoughts to stay patient and methodical. He couldn't move too quickly, nor could he wait too long. Within two hours, Pima Jack would take over the watch, and there would be no turning any trick on that half-Indian. Gil was younger and more resilient than the others, but he was tired too, restless as any fretful child; he hated routine with a passion, Wye knew, and before long, his boredom would be acute. Then his attention would start to wander. . . .

Wye let his nearly closed eyes shuttle to Pima Jack's blanket-wrapped form in the firelight. It was the half-breed's

122

animal-keen senses that worried him most. He wouldn't stand a prayer unless he got his hands on a gun before Pima Jack was roused. And then he'd have to take him out fast.

Briefly, Wye's glance moved on to his father. Again he felt a quiet wonderment that the longtime rift between Poe and himself had healed with the touch of a few words and the mildest of understandings. For they were still two different men, and that wouldn't change; yet all the rancor this fact had once generated was gone. They could have been friends now, except for two stubbornly opposed sets of values.

The waiting grew heavy in Wye's belly. He could see Gil starting to fidget, his watchfulness fraying with the slow trickle of time; it wouldn't be long. Wye tensed his muscles and rehearsed his moves: he had sized up the heap of broken limbs and twigs piled near the fire for fuel, and now his gaze sought one fat, sturdy-looking chunk of bough the thickness of a man's arm. It would do.

At last Gil's chin bowed to his chest. His head jerked half-up a couple of times, but it was only a drowsy reflex. Soon he was gently snoring. *Now,* Wye thought. A man sleeping in an uncomfortable posture slept lightly; he might snap awake any minute.

Wye eased the folds of the blanket apart and stretched sideways on his belly, twisting and inching painstakingly along the cold ground till he could close his fist around the end of the thick branch. He lifted himself to one knee, then swiftly stood and circled the fire, balancing his weight on his toes.

A burning chunk crumbled in the fire, this sound bringing his brother's head up. His eyes snapped open. Wye was already at his side; Gil's startled eyes were lifting as Wye swept down his clubbed bough in a short and savage arc. Gil's Stetson crumpled under the blow and he began falling forward. Wye yanked the rifle free before his brother's weight could cover it. He whipped around almost in the same moment, levering the weapon.

He hadn't expected time to get the drop; he was right. The slight noise he'd made in buffaloing Gil had brought Pima Jack lunging out of his blankets, clawing at the pistol in his belt. With no time to aim, Wye sent one blind shot at the half-breed and then pivoted and ran for the bordering woods. Pima Jack's pistol roared twice, but he was snap-shooting by firelight. Wye reached the edge of the natural clearing where the camp lay. Here he fell to a crouch and turned his rifle on the camp. His nerves were cool; he pulled another bead on the most dangerous one, Pima Jack. But the half-breed was already fading into the brush on the opposite side of the clearing. Even as he pulled trigger, Wye knew he'd missed.

Dundie, Dandy Mack, Yarbrough, and Poe were all rolling out of their blankets now, and Smoky was on her feet crying Gil's name as she ran toward his slumped form. Knowing he was momentarily screened by the brush and semi-darkness, Wye took time for a careful aim as Dundie hurried toward the fire, yelling questions. Wye fired three times, Dandy Mack yelled and fell to his knees, dropping his pistol. Dundie's gun went off as he fell, grabbing his leg. He pitched across the fire, giving a hoarse thin wail as his body smothered the blazing coals. For a moment the night rushed into the clearing, and then Dundie, howling, thrashed frantically away from the fire and it leaped high. Smoky had fallen across Gil's body.

Yarbrough had run forward, pumping shots at Wye's gunflash. He'd braced to a stop, his thick legs set apart, as the fire winked out. Now as the darkness washed back again he shot once more into the brush. The slug skimmed a little over Wye's head, clipping off a leaf that dropped on his shoulder. He set his sights on Ben's wide chest, but hesitated and then held his fire.

For Poe was on his feet and, his bound hands clenched tight against his belly, came powering at Yarbrough's back, his head and big shoulders bunched together. His full weight hit Ben in the small of the back with the force of a battering ram, and Ben crashed to the ground with Poe toppling solidly across his body.

"Wyatt!" Poe roared, pinning flat on his face. "Run, boy—run, damn you! It's no good! That breed'll get you sure! Don't—" His words ended in a grunt as Ben, heaving wildly under his weight, threw Poe sideways and rolled him off. Poe grabbed at Ben's pistol. He could put up a clumsy fight at best, with his wrists tied, but he kept his hold on the pistol and wrestled Yarbrough onto his back before Ben

124

yanked the gun free. He slammed it across Poe's temple in a chopping vicious blow, and Poe went limp.

Yarbrough was hotly swearing as he rolled Poe away and started to his feet. Wye sent a snap shot at him and missed, and Pima Jack opened up then from somewhere in the brush across the clearing, forcing Wye to melt back into the trees and darkness.

Deep in the brush he dropped back to his haunches and waited, listening. Yarbrough was thrashing around in the brush himself, now yelling Pima Jack's name, but the half-breed was too canny to answer. No doubt he'd be ferreting out every sound, analyzing its meaning and source, and it was likely he had traced by ear Wye's retreat into the brush and pinpointed his fresh position. When he came, Wye knew, he would come like a shadow.

Wye thought his best hope, and it seemed thin enough, was to stay absolutely motionless. The heavy cover rose black and impenetrable on every side of him; a pale half-moon made a feeble play of light through the network of twigs and leaves overhead. It was likely the half-breed could be on him before he had a hint of his coming, and Wye remembered that Pima Jack had a hunting knife as well as his pistol. He wondered which it would be. *He might be a middling-to-fair shot, but I'll bet he's a wizard with that knife.*

Wye rubbed his sweating palm on his coat; he felt the hard tangle of the cord that had bound his wrists outline through his pocket. The glimmer of an idea came to him. Maybe it wouldn't narrow the odds by much, but a desperate man couldn't ignore the finest advantage. Wye silently laid down his rifle and took out the cord. By feel, he partly disentangled its cunning arrangements of loops and knots that Pima Jack had used in securing his hands. Without a knife he could only get slack in the cord by loosening a few knots with his teeth and pulling out the loops. This gave him a little over two feet of still-tangled line, not nearly enough for safety. But it would have to do. With painstaking care he fastened one end of the cord to a stem of bush near his face, then flattened out on his belly.

Holding the other end looped around the fingers of one hand, gripping his rifle in the other hand, Wye crawled

125

sidelong away from the bush. He worked along this way by inches, and every crackle of a twig under his body made him freeze. He hadn't an idea of where the half-breed was by now, but he must be close.

Yarbrough had quit shouting and was trying to move more quietly through the woods. But Wye could easily pick up his movements, and he knew Ben was somewhere well off to his left, which made no problem just yet.

Wye slithered on his belly for about two yards, keeping the arm that anchored him to the cord flung out straight from his body. He came to a stop when he felt the cord draw taut; he stayed that way, utterly still now. Some men could see surprisingly well in the night, and Pima Jack was probably one. Wye only hoped that the clot of leaves and branches above his prone body would hide him.

He strained his ears; cold sweat seemed to puddle between his shoulder blades, or maybe it was only the chill crawling along his spine. He was counting on picking up something, any faintest sound, to tell him when the half-breed was close by. An eternity pulsed by in the dense slugging of his heart against his eardrums. *Nothing.*

There . . . a scraping whisper that might have been a man's sleeve grazing a leafy branch. Wye stared with an aching intensity at the patch of blackness under the trees from where the sound had seemed to come. Again there was the waiting, his nerves crawling with tension now, but there was no other sound, no movement. Maybe it had been a trick of his imagination—or Pima Jack was being careful. *If he is there and thinks I heard him, he'll wait for my nerve to crack. He'll expect as much. Yes, that has to be it; he's waiting. All right—*

Wye yanked the taut cord, shaking the bush. The instant he did, the darkness he was watching bloomed with powderflame. Pima Jack's pistol crashed four times, riddling the foliage. Wye let out a trailing groan and pulled the cord as tight as he could; the brush crackled and snapped as if a body had sagged into it.

The half-breed lunged with a cat's silent swiftness across a break in the woods, his lifted knife streaking with moonflash, to make sure of his kill. Wye leaped to his feet, sweeping the rifle level. He hadn't time to raise it more than hip-high before he pulled trigger. Pima Jack pivoted hard and fast with a grunt of surprise; Wye had missed him clean. And now Pima Jack was coming at him like a darting shadow, and Wye frantically worked the rifle.

The half-breed's long arm swung as he came into Wye, and Wye heard cloth rip and felt the slashing blow on his bicep. In the same moment, almost by reflex as Pima Jack's chest slammed against his rifle muzzle, Wye jerked the trigger again. The half-breed's light body was flung backward as if an unseen fist had smashed him. He doubled up on the ground, clutching his belly. His shirt was smoking; a moan gurgled from him.

Dimly, as it all happened, Wye had been aware of Yarbrough's heavy crashing advance through the brush to his rear. The shots had been bound to bring his stepfather to the spot, and Wye was mentally braced for the meeting. Yet for fleeting seconds, with a man dying at his feet, a wash of stunned reaction paralyzed Wye: he stood shaking, unable to move. Now somebody else was coming through the brush quartering straight for him; a voice he knew was calling his name, and that snapped the paralysis.

"Pa!" He yelled it at the top of his lungs. "Stay back!"

Poe plunged into the narrow break between the trees, in the same instant Yarbrough did. Both men came to a dead stop in the feeble moonlight. Wye's heart was choked in his throat, full of a cold fear for his father and nothing else. For Poe would be helpless with his hands tied—and unarmed. Even as that thought crossed his mind, Wye was bringing up the gun to bear on Yarbrough's thick chest. But in the rush of fear through him, his hands felt cold and heavy.

"Right here, Ben—" he heard his father say, and Yarbrough spun tightly to face him.

"Damn you, Poe," Yarbrough half-screamed. "God damn you to hell!"

He had seen what Wye only caught now, a glint of light racing along a pistol barrel. Poe's hands were still bound together, but they were coming up with a gun.

Yarbrough had just finished turning, his rifle braced to shoot, when Poe's bullet hit him. He folded in the middle like a doll broken in half, and his rifle went off at the sky. It was a reflex pulling of the trigger, no more; his body held a sprawling looseness as he hit the ground.

Wye's legs felt numb and alien as he moved forward,

127

halting before he quite reached Yarbrough. His stepfather's body was only a dark and anonymous lump on the forest loam under a branch-fretted moon, and he didn't feel anything in particular.

He felt his father move up beside him. Poe said quietly, "Well, boy, I knew you had it in your head to try something. Just never thought you'd be damnfool enough to go through with whatever." He roughened his voice against a slight break. "Not and take on five of 'em, for Christ's sake."

Wye shook his head and only then looked fully at his father. "It only started that way—five to one. Then it was five against two Lockharts. That made all the difference."

Poe growled, "Just cut these damn ropes off."

Wye got Pima Jack's knife and cut Poe's hands. "Thought Ben laid you out cold."

"He fetched me a pretty hard crack was all. I played possum till he went after you, then got my hands on Gil's Colt and waited for a sound I could follow up." Without more words Poe turned and plunged back through the trees toward the camp. Wye came after him, gripping his own arm just above the long slash Pima Jack's knife had made. He was bleeding hard; the whole arm of his coat was wet and slick.

Dandy Mack was in bad shape. One of Wye's bullets had shattered the bone of his right forearm, and he'd simply passed out. Dundie lay on his side by the fire, both hands grabbing his blood-soaked leg which was drawn up to his chest. His rifle lay near him, but he made no move toward it and Poe and Wye came into the firelight. He was hurt badly enough to need help, and he'd only get it from them. Dundie knew it, and he wasn't resisting.

Smoky still lay partly across Gil's unconscious form as she had fallen, and Wye thought she must have fainted. He watched Poe bend down and turn her over, and then he saw how the bullet had taken her in mid-run. Very gently, Poe raised her in his arms and stood up, and looked at Dundie. "Good shooting, Clem."

Dundie's face was ashen. "I didn't know." He nodded at Wye. "It was his shot in my leg that did it. I pulled the trigger unwittingly. A wild shot, pure accident—"

"Shut up," Poe said. He carried the girl to her blankets and laid her thin light body on one of them, and covered her

128

with the other. He spoke so softly that Wye barely caught his words: "Poor little kid. She never had any kind of chance. Best this way. She couldn't have known what hit her."

He walked back to Gil and knelt, no gentleness in his hands as he rolled his son on his back and pulled off his crushed hat. There was a great angling bruise across Gil's temple. He made a sound. Poe said, "He's all right," and started to get up when his eyes narrowed on Wye's bloody sleeve.

"Didn't see that before. The breed do that?"

Wye nodded. "Not too bad."

"The hell it ain't. You're bleeding like a stuck pig. I'll clean it and tie it off for you. Then there's some burying to be done." Poe paused bleakly. "It'll be a long night, I reckon."

CHAPTER EIGHTEEN

Wye came awake suddenly in the pre-dawn hours. He blinked at the gray sky, trying to think where he was. Then he remembered, and his empty hand stabbed in scared reflex for the gun he'd gone to sleep holding. It was gone. Now he smelled frying bacon and fresh coffee and sat up, pushing his blankets away. Poe was kneeling by the fire, back to him, stirring up the coals under a skillet and coffeepot.

"No need looking for your hogleg," Poe said without glancing around. "I got it. Chucked all the other guns out in the brush, so don't look for them either."

Wye climbed gingerly to his feet. He felt a little feverish but strong enough. His arm, bulky with the bandages Poe had put on, gave only a faint twinge, but it was stiff. Poe had torn up a shirt to make a sling for it. So far it hadn't given Wye any trouble, except that it was useless at a time when he badly wanted two good arms.

Wye sank down on his haunches by the fire. He said

129

dourly, "I suppose it was like taking candy from a little kid."

"Just about. When a body gets banged up, nature just puts him to sleep no matter how hard he tries keeping awake." Poe fed small sticks into the blaze. "You must be all hell-afire to take your brother back to that noose that'll be waiting for him."

Wye glanced over toward Gil and the two wounded men who were still asleep. He said bitterly, "It's great for a son to find out what'll take his pa's favor. I should have robbed a few trains and killed a sheriff or two. I'd have been in solid."

"Sure," Poe murmured, "he's in solid. That's why I got him tied up under that blanket. Him and Dundie both."

"Hurrah," Wye said. "Afraid they won't go with you to Mexico willingly?"

"You can fetch Dundie and the two hundred thousand back to your grandpaw. Tell him they're a present from me. But I'm taking your brother with me, and I won't stand still for anyone who gets in my way."

"All this has a familiar ring," Wye said wearily. "I guess there's no more to say."

"Not a lot." Poe's gaze softened a little. "You done all by your duty that any man could. Let it go, can't you?"

"No." Wye's voice shook. "Pa, look at it straight. You'll get him down in Mexico—then what? You can't keep him tied up forever. And once he's loose, how'll you control him? He won't stay by you after this. What'll you do then?"

"Ain't figured that much ahead, but I'll tell you one thing." Poe shoved a last twig in the fire, then came to his feet, his eyes like greenish slate. "Your brother ain't for hanging, boy. You can tie to that, because I say that's how it'll be, come hell or high water."

Wye gave a dull nod. "I'd agree it's quite possible he won't *hang*. But would you do one thing?"

"What is it?"

"Just ask him if he has any regrets about killing Clete Landrum—any at all."

Poe's face was expressionless. He took the skillet and coffeepot off the fire, then roused out Gil and Dandy Mack and Dundie. After a hasty breakfast, Poe lost no time breaking camp. He'd spent most of last night excavating a trench and burying the bodies of Yarbrough and Smoky and

130

Pima Jack under the largest boulders he could lift. All that remained now was to clean a few utensils and douse the fire and pack the gear, then saddle four horses and drive off the extra ones.

Afterward, with the three gunmen tied in their saddles, Poe handed Wye back the pistol he'd taken from him. "You'll be needing this to take Clem in. It's empty, and you'll have kind of a time loading it with one arm stiffed up. Time you're done, we'll have a head start."

Wye took the Colt and dropped it in his holster. "I'm in no shape to object," he murmured. "But I mean to tell McKelvey everything. You understand me? I'll tell him where I last saw you and what I know of your plans, and he'll try to head you off short of the border."

Poe said, "Sure," his tone neither censuring nor friendly. "We can shake hands anyway."

Wye gripped his hand, and their eyes locked, and the strangeness between them was gone. They were two men set at grim odds because each had to act according to his own lights—but the old breach between them was healed for good.

Wye stood in the little clearing and watched them ride out south, his father and his brother, till they were swallowed in the trees. Then he stepped into his saddle and put his horse back down the trail they'd come by yesterday, Dundie's and Dandy Mack's horses following on leadropes.

They rode steadily through the morning and into the afternoon, making fairly good time. The stress of horsebacking with their wounds had the two outlaws feverish and, Wye suspected, in a good deal of pain, though neither of them voiced a complaint. Wye didn't feel in the best of fettle himself; the roughness of the trail had set up a steady, pounding ache from his shoulder to his fingers, and there was a faint, incessant, maddening buzz in his ears.

Toward late afternoon he picked up the first sound of horses coming beyond a bend in the canyon trail. He thought it might be another trick of his humming ears, but he wasn't taking chances. Dropping off his horse, he pulled his gun and moved quickly to the canyon bend hugging its flank, ready to take a defensive position here.

Then he halted, blinking against the sullen dance of heat and flinty brightness on the bare rocks. The four riders were

131

McKelvey and his three Parkinson men. He stepped out to hail them.

"Your grandpa was plenty worried on your account, young fellow," McKelvey told him when they were all off their horses and resting and smoking in the shadow of the rimrock. "When you weren't back by morning after taking the money to the place indicated, he put us on the trail. We went over the spot and found something specific to follow up, for once: your tracks and those of the man who took you. It was slow going at first, but once we'd followed the sign to Dundie's camp by the caves, tracking your party was no problem. Not knowing how many of 'em there might be, we couldn't be sure, from the number of horses, whether or not Dundie had kept his word to return Miss Chaney and the boy. But you say he did. All right, what's the rest of it? What's happened?"

Wye told it all, his voice dull and wooden. He watched the ground between his feet as he talked. When he lifted his head, he felt the penetrating brightness of McKelvey's eyes. "Your arm's bleeding," the old detective said.

Wye looked blankly at the spreading red stain on his bandage. "It's nothing."

"Want me to look at it?"

"Not necessary."

McKelvey watched him for a long moment, something close to compassion in his lined face. "Kicking yourself won't help anything, boy," he said quietly.

"What do you mean?"

"Why, just that you're hating your own guts because you had to tell us the truth about your pa and brother. You could have covered for 'em any number of ways—you could have said both of 'em were killed last night and you had buried 'em along with Yarbrough and the girl and the half-breed. Instead, you maybe told us enough to fetch them up cold before they reach the border. You think you'd be hating yourself any less if you hadn't done your duty and told us what really happened? Don't bet on it, boy." McKelvey's tone held a familiar dryness. "Duty. I've been serving that particular taskmistress all my life, and she sinks the spurs hard. You think I don't know? Take off your shirt. I'm going to look at that arm."

Wye did as he was told. McKelvey cleaned the wound

132

and rebandaged it, while two of his men did the same for both outlaws. Afterward McKelvey squatted on his heels and pulled a map from his pocket and spread it open. "We're here." He tapped the map, then moved his finger downward. "And Lockhart and his son will be crossing to the border by this route."

Dundie had some of his color back and he was puffing on a cigar. He took it from his mouth and said with satisfaction, "I planned it that way, ye ken. The trails holds to rugged and unsettled country all the way."

"Very astute," McKelvey said. "But it's a way that would have run you into a trap if somebody figured out what you had in mind, as I did. Here." He ran an arcing finger across the map. "Anybody as much as a day behind you could leave your trail at this point—and circle—and cut across your line of travel just a few miles above the border. It's a good deal farther that way, but it's clear and open country—we could cut your time in half."

Dundie puffed his cigar, nodding ruefully. "I'm inclined to hand ye that game, McKelvey. Not that it's any matter now."

"It is to Poe Lockhart," McKelvey said grimly. He got to his feet, pocketing the map. "Let's get moving. We can be at the south end of San Lomas Pass by sunset tomorrow. He'll have to come that way through the hills."

Wye began, "I'm going to go with—"

"You're not," McKelvey cut in. "We'll be riding hard and fast for the next thirty hours. You wouldn't last two hours at the pace I mean to set. And you have a prisoner to take in. Do your duty, sheriff." He paused. "We'll try to take 'em alive, but you know I can't promise a damned thing."

Wye knew. He watched the detectives ride away down the canyon. Then he helped Dundie and Dandy Mack back into their saddles, and the three of them moved on.

Wye doggedly held the saddle deep into the twilight, and would have kept on except that his brain was getting as fuzzy as the beige blur of dusk pressing around them. They made a dry and fireless camp; none of them wanted to eat, and after hobbling out the horses and tying up his prisoners for the night, Wye drifted into a sweaty and fitful sleep. Toward morning the mild fever and chills left him, and his sleep was even and untroubled then.

The sun was high when he woke. He lay quietly on his back, blinking at the sky, his thoughts crisp and clear. The troubles weren't ended—maybe in some ways they had just started—but he knew what he must do and that he could face whatever came out of it. He wasn't afraid any more: maybe that was the best certainty a man could hope for in this whole troubled business of living. He'd made a brave speech to Poe about following his own star, but only now was he really bracing to meet the harsh demands that his decision would make of him.

It was sunset when rode into Leedstock. He was hungry, dirty and unshaved; he was half-dead for a full night's sleep in a bed, and his arm needed a doctor's attention. Yet he took only the time to leave his prisoners, both of them in deep fever now, at Doc Phelps' and turn the horses in at the livery barn, before heading for a small frame house on a shady block just off the main street.

Tacey answered his tug on the bell-pull. She opened the door, and for a moment she only looked at him. She stood clean and slim in starched calico, her hair shining in the dim hallway, and his name whispered from her lips.

"Wye. Oh thank God—"

She came with a sigh into his arms, not caring about the dirt or bloodstains or his haggard condition. She held him tightly, and he felt her trembling.

Tacey drew him into the parlor where a lamp was already burning on low flame against the early twilight, and then she saw the dirty bandage on his arm. "What's that?"

"Just a cut. Tace—"

"Let me change the bandage." She started toward the kitchen, but Wye took her by the arms and turned her to face him.

"Tacey . . . listen. It was Gil who shot your dad. My brother did it and I was there and I saw him do it—and I didn't tell you."

He dropped his hands from her arms. Tacey did not stir; her eyes in the lampglow were very dark and full of changing lights, and yet her face altered only faintly. "Then why tell me now? Why tell anybody now? Did it change anything to wait this long?"

"No. I guess the only thing that's changed is my thinking." He lifted his hands slightly and let them drop.

134

"At first I told myself I was protecting Gil. That was bad enough—and then I got to realizing that I'd mostly kept quiet for fear of losing you. And that was even worse."

"Why?" she said softly. "Because you were human enough to be afraid? Because you might have been putting a brother you cared for ahead of those brittle standards of yours? Are you truly ashamed of that?"

"Not the way I was, I guess. Or I couldn't have come here to face you—and tell you—"

"But you did come, you did tell me—that's what's important. Oh Wye! I tried to tell you that day by the river—I'm not perfect, and I couldn't spend my life with a man who thought he was and that everybody else should be."

"I still believe in the letter of the law," Wye said slowly. "I still think I was wrong not telling you about Gil. That I failed in my duty as an officer to boot."

"So do I. But I might have done the same in your place—so might anybody who's human enough. Just don't be ashamed of being human, Wye!"

"I won't be again," he said gravely. "I was going to tell you that too. And a lot more, Tacey—"

"But that will wait." She pressed her fingers against his lips and moved back into his arms.

CHAPTER NINETEEN

Poe took one backward look at the narrow clearing where Wye was, and a wrenching regret ran through him. Years ago he'd lost this same son, but the loss had been so gradual, he could remember no pain. This time was a lot different, for this time he'd lost Wye just as they'd touched the threshold of understanding.

The trees closed behind Gil and him, and Poe set his eyes dead front. He couldn't afford to be occupied by any thoughts except getting Gil to safety. He silently computed the miles between here and the Mexican border, and

135

judged that, allowing for a night stop, a strong and steady clip would bring them out of the San Lomas Pass above the border sometime late tomorrow.

For almost the first time since last evening, Gil softly spoke: "Now we're on our way, how about taking off this rope? And giving back my guns?"

"I chucked 'em in the brush. You're out a couple guns." It was only partly true; he had cached all the outlaws' weapons, including Gil's rifle, in some thickets where they could rust for all he cared. But he'd kept Gil's pistol, the well-balanced Colt that had killed Yarbrough, stashing it in his saddlebags against any emergency. So much for an outlaw's caution. His own pistol, the one that had been Tom Rydell's, was holstered at his hip, and Rydell's Winchester was in the boot under his knee.

Gil said, "How about taking off this goddamn rope, then?"

"Later."

Gil cursed him. "What good you think you're doing by this? How long you figure you can hold onto me?"

"No good at all," Poe said woodenly. "It's something I got to do, that's all. And I'll hold onto you, all right. You might's well shut up, boy. Talking's no good either."

"That's right!" Gil half-shouted. "So cut me loose and let me go my way. You can go back and get off scot-free for the way you cut all our throats, can't you?" The wildness and protest flared higher in his face. "Let me go, Pa! We ain't alike any more, you and me. You got to be like Wye—him and you always tryin' to be a goddamn conscience to me. You go your way . . . let me go mine."

"I told you to shut up."

They rode without any more talk through the morning and far into the afternoon and early evening. Both men were slumped with exhaustion when Poe called a halt on a silky-grassed meadow cupped like a green pearl in this vast, arching upheaval of rocky hills and semi-desert where they hadn't crossed a sign of human habitation.

Poe set to the camp jobs, hobbling out the horses and building the fire. He didn't bother to bind his son's hands again after untying them from the saddle horn. He had the guns, and he judged that Gil was too worn down by the long

136

day to offer any trouble. Also he figured that his son would soon probably be ready to listen to reason, as it became obvious he couldn't gain a thing by fighting Poe's will.

When he'd cooked up a few provisions and they were sitting by the fire wolfing down their supper, Poe broke the long silence. "Hope you're starting to see sense, boy. I didn't like cutting Clem's throat like I done, but I'd of done a sight more to get you away from him. It's no life worth the having—I ought to know that better'n anyone, and time you started seeing it too." Poe paused to isolate his next words. "What's past is done with. We're heading for Mexico because it's a place we can start over. Won't be easy no ways, strange country and all, and two of us together'll have the most chance. You ought to see that. I don't want to bulldoze you, boy; I just want you alive and making sense to yourself. Hear me?"

Gil was staring at the fire, and he didn't lift his eyes. "I hear you."

"What do you say?"

"Do I got any choice?"

Poe picked up a chunk of wood and tossed it on the fire. "Not a damn one."

"That's how I see it." Gil let his shoulders lift and fall in the faintest of shrugs. "Looks like we go the same way, then." His voice reflected an utter indifference; he raised his tin cup and took a deep swig of coffee, draining the cup. He spat out the dregs and said, "What about some more java?"

"All right." Poe felt a perceptible relaxing in the tightness of his belly. At least Gil was coming to his senses; he was resigning himself at least, and that could only be a good sign—time would take care of the rest.

Casually Gil reached for the small, battered coffeepot by the edge of the fire. He lifted it in the same idle way, but suddenly then he pivoted on his heels and swung the pot back and forward, and let go at Poes's head.

Taken completely off guard, Poe just managed to fling up an arm and partly block the blow. The pot bounced off his hunched shoulder, the coffee spraying across his neck. The liquid was no longer scalding, but hot enough to numb Poe's muscles with the brief, agonizing shock of contact. A few seconds, no more, but enough time for Gil to be on his feet

137

scooping up the iron skillet, then come diving across the fire to swing it against Poe's skull. The blackness was instant and total.

When Poe came to, he was sprawled on his belly and face as he had fallen. His cheek was ground against the earth; his whole body was stiff with cold. He turned his head achingly sideways till he saw the fire with its last cherry coals winking out. He must have been out cold for hours. It was pitch dark and the moon was high, he saw by turning his head farther; it must be close to midnight, give or take an hour.

He sat slowly up, fighting the ragged waves of pain and sickness. Then he bent sideways and vomited thoroughly. Climbing to his feet, he felt better, even if his head contained the effect of getting split by an ax-blow. He touched it tenderly and found the hair of his temple matted with dried blood.

Gil was gone, of course. Poe bent gingerly and with a stick stirred up the fire's dim glow enough to take stock of his situation. The utensils and provisions were gone; so were his rifle and pistol. His saddle and saddlebags and blanket still lay where he had dropped them. His horse stood to one side of the clearing, softly whickering. Its hobble was gone, and he supposed that Gil to forestall pursuit had turned the animal loose and driven him off. But the horse couldn't have gone far, and Poe was glad that he had occupied so many idle hours in coddling and petting the animal: he knew a master.

Forgetting the wicked ache of his head in a driving rage to get moving, Poe took only time enough to dig out his spare pistol—Gil's—and ram it in his belt before saddling up. He kicked sand over the fire, then stepped into the saddle and turned south through the night toward San Lomas Pass.

Gil had three to four hours' start on him, and Gil would be moving briskly but not in a blind hurry, since he would believe he'd cut off any possibility of a close pursuit by Poe. Weighing these things, Poe thought that by pushing hard he should overhaul Gil sometime tomorrow.

And then what? The thought made its inevitable flicker somewhere at the core of his insensate determination. He shoved the hopeless query savagely out of sight again. *He's my son—Gil is my son.*

138

The blackness passed into gray; a pearly dawn came at last, and the sun climbed. By mid-morning Poe was deep in San Lomas Pass, picking his way slowly over the rock-strewn floor and fretting with impatience. Yet he knew that if not for this delay that couldn't be helped, he'd be tempted to let the horse out to a killing pace. The animal was almost to the end of his tether as it was, and Poe wasn't in much better shape himself. He was still dizzy and sick from the blow, and he was too damned old for this sort of boy's game. But he could hang on grimly because he had a reason: always the final key to a man's strength.

Noon came and passed; the sun began heeling over toward the west. By late afternoon Poe was still steadily riding, or at least holding the saddle in a fog of exhaustion. All he cared was that Gil was somewhere up ahead. From his old faint memory of San Lomas Pass, the end of it wasn't far now. If he didn't catch up with Gil before he was out of the pass, trailing him from there on would be almost impossible.

Poe suddenly reined in, the weariness draining out of him. Somebody was shooting up ahead, the shots making a thin rataplan of stony echoes that caromed off the cliffs. He listened for a moment, then set his spurs and drove his horse in a savage run toward the last bend in the pass. Veering around a cliff's curving flank, he saw the mouth of the pass yawn wide just ahead.

A man—he knew it was Gil—was crouched behind a shoulder of rock, firing with a blunt, dogged rhythm at the other men who were laid up in cover out in the boulder-studded plain beyond the pass. Poe didn't have to guess about what had happened. Wye had gotten to McKelvey and his Parkinsons and tipped them off, or else old Boiler Britches had figured things out for himself. Either way, by information or a reasonable guess, he had worked south by the fastest way to head off the fugitives at the terminus of the San Lomas. There must have been an unlooked-for hitch in the deadfall—Gil had sensed something amiss, or one of the Parks had made a wrong move—and now it was a dead stand-off, if four guns against one was a stand-off.

Four against two Lockharts now, Poe grimly amended, and dropped off his mount. He pulled his pistol from his belt as he sprinted forward. "Gil—"

139

The roar of gunfire and Gil's dogged concentration on his enemies had smothered Poe's arrival. He saw Gil's shoulders jerk in surprise, and then he came wheeling around on his haunches. His face was a snarling and sweat-creased mask of hate that made Poe pull up dead in his tracks. Gil's mouth formed an obscenity; he yelled, "I told you to let me alone, Goddamn you!" He swung his rifle to bear, working the lever savagely.

"No! No, for God's sake, boy!" Poe hard himself yelling hoarsely, and then the rifle was coming level on his chest, and the wild and feral intent in his son's action was beyond question.

Poe had a split-second to aim and snap off his shot. The bullet's impact in Gil's shoulder flung him on his back. The hurt didn't remotely brake his savagery of the moment; he rolled over and came scrambling up, still gripping the rifle. His eyes glared at Poe; he was fighting pain to bring up the rifle and steady it.

Gil had rolled far enough away from the sheltering rock to expose himself. And even as he came lunging back on his feet, the detectives were opening fire. A bullet took him between the shoulders, its smashing force arching him forward and then dropping him in a limp, spraddled fall. It was over just that quickly.

Poe's raised arm sank to his side. The gun fell from his fingers and he did not know it. His legs were rubbery, but they carried him to Gil's side. He dropped on a knee and rolled his son's body over. The bullet had gone clean through him, straight into the heart, and there was only a little bleeding on his shirt. Even that was quickly checked, caked with dirt now, and drying.

He heard men's boots, and a dim reflex pulled his eyes up to the four detectives coming toward him. This meant nothing, and he looked back at his son's relaxed young face, his dead young face, and thought how strangely clean it looked in spite of the dirt streaking it.

The ride back to Leedstock would be a long, long one. So they buried Gil Lockhart not far from where he had fallen. All of them helped deepen the grave in the stony ground, but Poe himself wrapped his son's body in blankets and laid him in the shallow trough. They filled it with rocks; he lashed a couple of sticks crosswise and set the crude marker at the head of the mound. And he stood there a long time while the detectives drew off a ways to rest and have a smoke.

The setting sun had begun to flame orange and pink along the gray rimrock. McKelvey came over to stand beside him and say, "Well, it didn't do a lot of good, all the trouble you took, did it? You ought to know why." His voice was thin and old and tired, and there was no bite to it. "No matter how things went, Lockhart, no matter what you'd done, it had to end something like this. Sooner or later it would have ended this way."

Poe rasped a hand over the black scrub of whiskers on his jaw. He only nodded, thinking with an obscure calm, *That's right*. Because for some time, after all, he'd known in the back of his mind the truth of what McKelvey was saying now. There was no longer anything to prevent him from confessing it outright. Gil was dead, and so he could admit the whole truth to himself and know, even as he did, that if he had it all to do over he would have done no differently.

McKelvey said, "There are no perfect answers any of us know of. Maybe there are no answers anywhere. Funny, though—how we're made so we have to go on acting exactly as if there were. Guess that's the great flaw in man's nature. And in a strange kind of way, the great glory in it too." He dropped a hand on Poe's shoulder. The oddness of this gesture from old Boiler Britches caused Poe to turn his head.

"No reason now," McKelvey said, "for you not to swallow a little more time in Coldrock, is there?"

Poe said, "Thanks," in a voice dull with indifference.

"I mean two-three years, at the most. You have no reason not to play it straight down the line from here on, and I can think of no reason not to see you get the chance. I still owe you my half of a bargain—it needs paying off. I'll make up a cover story for what happened here—it'll boil down to you were helping us—and my boys will back my word. We'll all tell it that way in court."

Poe shook his head wearily. "Wyatt knows that I was helping Gil get away. He'll never go along with you.

"Don't be so damned sure," McKelvey said dryly. "And give him some credit. He's still got some growing up to do, but he's been coming along fast of late. As for Dundie, and Dandy Mack, their word won't count against all of ours. And even if Wye doesn't go along—well, I have the governor's ear, and he owes me a couple of favors. Old Fancher isn't without influence either, and he should be duly grateful for the recovery of his gold—thanks to you. No matter how much time you collect, I wouldn't be a damn bit surprised if there's an early pardon for the man that broke up Dundie's bunch. Now if you're done here, Lockhart, let's get mounted. There are a few hours of daylight left, and I want to use them."

Mounted, the five men rode out of the pass, one of the detectives leading Gil's horse. Poe looked back just once at the mound of rocks in the darkening gorge, then set his eyes ahead.

He still owed McKelvey a word, but that grave would stay in the front of his mind for a long time. It was too early for him to voice the thanks that needed saying without his choking on them. Later, maybe, the words would come easier.

Later. . .